Didn't Know I Was Lost: Stories

By Warren Pete

For my family.

Stories

Underneath It All: Inspired by True Events

Day Six

By the time Brandon woke up, it was 1:29PM, the sun was already past its peak, and it was too late to do any good. Brandon had signed up to volunteer for a food drive held at a nearby homeless shelter that started at eight in the morning and ended over an hour ago. Oh well, there was nothing Brandon could do about it and he wasn't going to beat himself up. So few students even bothered to sign up to volunteer and Brandon did so every week. He made it out to the homeless shelter about half the time, whenever other plans didn't come up or he wasn't out 'til 5AM the night before. He knew the shelter expected him to come every week, but this is college, he wanted his fun, too. Plus, it's poor planning to have charity events on Saturday morning, as if the poor, homeless, and needy can't wait a few more hours, despite being poor, homeless, and needy their whole lives.

It was 2:03PM when Brandon finally rolled out of Meg's bed and walked to the dorm's balcony. Meg, or Megla, was the girl he'd been seeing for a couple months. He didn't even bother listening to one of Meg's five voice messages; no doubt scolding him for missing the event, her event. He didn't care; he was pretty much over her by now. He put up with her *save the world* crap for a couple months now and if it wasn't for her letting him sleep over and cooking for him, he would be gone by now. Now all she does is bitch at him all day about them becoming "official," about him investing as much into the relationship as she is, but that's not going to happen. There's no way in Hell Brandon would ever commit to a relationship. He doesn't need Megla. She doesn't mean anything to him. There are plenty of foreign-exchange students like her that are dying to get with a big strong American, so Brandon would have no trouble finding one that wouldn't give him crap for not attending their pointless events.

Brandon got up, stretched, and walked into the bathroom. Even though waking up this late wasn't a rare occurrence, Brandon still never really knew whether he should eat breakfast or lunch. He wasn't even hungry; he'll wait 'til dinner. Brandon brushed his teeth with his electric toothbrush, only the best for his teeth. His pearly whites helped him get his girls and the toothpaste helped remove the taste of vomit from his mouth.

Damn, I'm hungover. Brandon dragged his feet to the kitchen. The place was a mess, nonetheless his own doing. It's probably best he eats something. The fridge was decently stocked: full of tandori (oven-baked wheat paste), muglai barata (bread with spicy meat), fried hilsa (Bangladeshi fish), and sandesh (milk- and sugar-based dessert). He only knew this because Meg labeled each food and wrote a brief description on each so Brandon could learn about her culture. If there was someone that should be learning about another culture, it should be Megla. She could learn how to make an American dish or two.

He scooped up all four plates and brought them over to the couch and turned on the TV. No surprise, it was set to the news, some other part of the world on fire, nothing to be done about it, a news station's source of livelihood found in the hours of repetitive commentary and "analysis." Scrolling through the channels, nothing but reality shows, golf, and reruns. Decided to settle on cartoons. It's been awhile since he's seen any; cartoons have changed a lot since he was growing up. In this one, the protagonist, a two-headed fish, was trying to lead a fight against a stray cat population, or something like that. No wonder kids are so messed up these days.

Brandon unwrapped all of the plates, bracing for the smell. Awful. He started off with the tandori, figuring it was the plainest dish, and the least likely to taste horrible. And it didn't have any of those spices; Brandon hates spice. It was unleavened and tasteless. So bland. Next was the muglai barata. Way too spicy, so spicy he needed to have another bite of bland tandori to get the spice out of his mouth. The hilsa was awful, he hated fish. The sandesh wasn't bad though, or it wasn't as bad as the other dishes, Brandon thought as he carried the plates back to the kitchen. *It's a shame Megla takes so much time to cook all this just for it to smell and taste like rotten garbage*, Brandon thought as he shoveled the remainder of the four near-full plates into the already overflowing trash. Most of the food slid over the excess and onto the floor. Brandon figured he better leave her dorm before she sees the mess he created.

Brandon sat back down at the couch, looking at his smartphone to try to order a pizza. Real food. Megla was calling right as Brandon was making his topping selections and he accidentally pressed "Answer." *Damn.*

"Hello."

"Where have you been?" Meg was pissed.

"I slept in."

"AHHHH!" Meg vented. "When did you wake up?"

"Like half an hour ago."

"Are you serious? I can't believe you slept through the entire event. This is the third event in a row you missed."

"Look, it's not like I meant to miss it."

"You know, you wouldn't be sleeping in so late if you stopped drinking so much. You're destroying yourself."

"Look, I did not pick up the phone to be lectured by you. I'm sorry I missed the event, but I'll come and help next time."

"Yeah, sure. Well I'm walking home right now and the mess you made from last night better be cleaned up."

"Yeah, yeah, don't worry about it." Brandon hung up before Megla could respond.

With the first trace of haste all day, Brandon got up and put on his pants from last night and one of Megla's unisex school sweatshirts and walked out the door. Brandon figured he better leave her dorm before she sees the mess he created. Her place was way too messy for him to clean it up. He'll just buy her flowers instead.

He grabbed his wallet and keys, and got the hell out of there. He decided to walk to Savers Super Mart. They had the cheapest flowers. They had the cheapest everything. And yes, they literally had everything: clothes, groceries, electronics, furniture, bikes, cigarettes, cars, caskets, pets, and even pet caskets.

There were a bunch of people protesting outside of Savers Super Mart. No surprises here. As a political science major, Brandon well knew that the low prices came at a price, and Savers Super Mart went to great lengths to protect their methods. It was evident in their classic commercials:

Uncle Savers Super Sam (decked in all patriotic attire): "And I guarantee you won't find a deal like this anywhere else."

Overweight 6-year old boy (standing with his loving family): "Gee that's great! But how do you get your prices so low?"

Uncle Savers Super Sam: "Sorry son, that's a secret."

Overweight 6-year old boy: "Awww, why?"

Uncle Savers Super Sam: "Well, sometimes things are best kept secret."

Overweight 6-year old boy: "Shucks, what if I find out?"

Uncle Savers Super Sam: "Son, if you find out, all these fun toys, and all these great prices will go away. We don't want that, do we?"

Overweight 6-year old boy: "Oh no sir, I'll never ask a question again."

Uncle Savers Super Sam: (pats boy on head) "That's a good boy. Now free candy for everyone!"

Brandon knew they didn't use the best business practices, and year after year were listed as one of the worst businesses in the world, but hey, they offered low prices, and he was a broke college student. If it wasn't for Savers Super Mart, there's no way he could afford the month-long trip to Europe he was planning.

The store was simple: a big open space filled with aisles and aisles of stuff. No decorations, no friendly staff, no color. Just plain white walls packed with stuff. Brandon always smiled here. As he progressed through his education as a business minor, he learned about the importance of customer service, attractive fixtures, and serving the community and how that all led to increased brand image and better sales. Yet here, in Savers Super Mart, they had none of that, yet were bigger than their top three competitors combined.

Even as a regular patron, it took Brandon a while to navigate the 360,000 square foot store. Over the next hour he picked up disposable razors, so he could clean up to hit the clubs in the big city tonight; golf balls, for his monthly 9-hole affair with his roommates; and finally, Brandon stopped by the clothing section.

It was a bit challenging for Brandon to find his way around the clothing section. The selection was mainly sizes XL and above, to fit the main shopping core. Even though Brandon was a good 20 pounds overweight since he quit his part-time construction job, he still was considered among the fittest in this place, another reason why he liked it so.

He picked out a blue collared shirt, some socks, and a sweatshirt. Brandon was on his way out when he saw this week's sale item—suit jackets. Brandon desperately needed one for some upcoming job interviews. He scooped up the first one he found in his size—a plain black suit jacket with four pockets. The suit's inner tag indicated that it was made in Megla's native Bangladesh. Perhaps this would earn Brandon some brownie points for supporting her homeland.

The total came out to $26, for all of that. Crazy. God bless America. God bless Savers Super Mart.

His pocket buzzed, he was getting called. Surprisingly not from Meg, it was from Cindy, a cute girl from class. She was Cambodian, or Vietnamese, or something like that.

"Hello?"

"Hi Brandon, it's Cindy." Brandon adored her meek voice.

"Oh, hey, Cindy..." even though Brandon knew full well who she was.

"Cindy Sok."

"Oh yes, yes. How's it going?"

"I'm good. Are you feeling better after yesterday?"

Brandon vaguely remembered how sick he got from the night before. "Yeah I'm fine."

"Good. I'm sorry, but I couldn't help but notice yesterday, but Megla was yelling at you last night for the longest time. I felt bad for you."

Now this, Brandon remembered clearly. Wasn't quite sure whether his head rang from all the alcohol or from the tirade Meg went on the night before. "Yeah, I hate how she treats me like a child sometimes. All the time."

"I know this isn't my place, but you deserve better than that."

"I think that a lot, sometimes."

"I can't believe you still put up with her."

"Well, to be honest, we're not really together anymore."

"Oh no!" Cindy said, half-heartedly. "What happened?"

"We kinda both saw we don't really belong together." A realization that only Brandon knew.

"Oh, that's too bad." A lie that they both knew. "As I said though, you deserve a lot better."

"Any suggestions?"

"Hmm, I think I might know a girl," she teased.

"Oh yeah?"

"Yeah. Come by my apartment on 53 Fenhill around 8 tonight and we'll see how I can treat you."

Brandon paused to calm himself. "That, that sounds good."

"Perfect, see you then." Cindy hung up.

Brandon couldn't repress his cheek-to-cheek grin, even while calling Megla to say he was moving on.

Day Five

It was Sunday night, and a handful of the most powerful people in the world were sitting around a pure gold table. The most powerful man in the world, Baron Hesson, paced around the room.

"Alright, alright, we're going to have a whole hailstorm of shit heading our way if we don't do something about this now! I don't know how the media found out about this, maybe none of the Kardashians got married or divorced today; but all I know is we have to clean it up! So we're going to go around the room until we find an idea that will get us out of this mess! So make this good because your job, YOUR LIFE depends on this. I'm going on Ron O'Hara in half an hour and I need to nail this." Hesson stopped, and stared across the table. "Alright, Margarita, your position was born out of nightmares like this, you go first."

Margarita Reyna, the Chief Officer of Corporate Responsibility, stood up. Reyna, a longtime leader of the Global Peace Troops Organization, left because she knew that helping all the people in the world wasn't going to pay for her 5 children's college educations. "Well, here's the angle, just like in Guatemala, this is not Savers Super Mart's fault. These were contractors hired by Savers Super Mart. They know our values and motto of saving costs at all costs and they pushed the issue onto safety, unprovoked by us. Regardless, we need to move fast, and move big. Just because Savers Super Mart isn't at fault, doesn't mean we don't care about the victims. Starting today, we will make a concerted push to improve all safety measures in every factory related to Savers Super Mart. That will mean full inspections of every facility. That will mean regular check-ups from fire marshals and health inspectors. With this plan, we will work all facilities to either conform to our demand, or we will take our business elsewhere. Because at Savers Super Mart, we may strive to save costs at all costs, but spare no expense to save human lives!"

Everyone turned to Hesson, who paused for a half second, "Brilliant plan, may need to pull back the reins on the spending on this project, but good work Margarita. What's this project called?"

Margarita, with a sudden gust of confidence from the CEO's support, exclaimed "Decrease Injuries Everywhere."

The board nodded approvingly until Gus Relaford, the Chief Marketing Officer, flailed his arms. "Wait, the initials for Decrease Injuries Everywhere is D-I-E, die!"

A gasp ran through the boardroom, Savers Super Mart was doomed. Margarita shrank back to her seat, defeated.

Gus stood, slicing through the panic, "how about Helping Eliminate Loss of People."

Pensive thoughts around the room.

Gus repeated, "Helping Eliminate Loss of People, H-E-L-P, help."

"Phenomenal! Marvelous save, Gus!"

Following the CEO's lead, everyone continued with the praise, even Margarita, who was noticeably bitter because she was not born a creative marketing genius like Gus.

"Now hold on a second," interjected Neil Kim, cueing a collective groan. Kim, the Chief Operations Officer, was a numbers mastermind, but known internally as the Chief Dream Executioner. "Even with this so-called name change, this program will be too extravagant. Just hearing Margarita's expenses, there will be an astronomical impact to our fixed costs, operating expenses, lower our profit margin, cut our-"

"Cut to the point please."

"This program will cost too much to implement."

"And your solution?"

"Well, the program's too expensive but it is a genius title and concept. Still, it's going to cost us billions."

"Now look," Hesson ordered, "we brought in $3.1 trillion in revenue last year, we could afford to put some muscle behind this program. There has to be a program we can cut to fund this. I mean this program can make the lives safer for millions of workers around the world and make us look good. There's plenty of programs we don't need."

"You're right Baron. Well, off the top of my head, we could cut the budget in half for the annual investor meeting. We can take out the performances by Beyoncé and the Rolling Stones and perhaps hold the meeting here in America versus holding it in Paris like last year."

"Woah woah woah," Baron interjected.

"But we love Beyoncé!" cried Gus.

Kim raised his hand to silence the group, sensing his position of power. "Well, we can keep the title and hollow out the actual program. Instead of taking time and money to set up the infrastructure behind all this, we can shoot a few commercials, create a logo, hold a few pretaped press conferences, and we emerge as a better company. The public will be satisfied and disinterested within the week."

"I'll be damned. You may be dull as a piece of hay, Kim, but you sure know how to save us money!"

"Thank you sir."

Kanta, Hesson's secretary, entered the office, "Sir?"

"Yes Kanta?"

"It's ten minutes to your interview, the crew is all set up in your office."

By the time Kanta finished her sentence, he was already on his way out the door. "Thanks Kanta, wish me luck, time to slay a UFO!"

O   O   O   O   O   O

Baron sat behind his desk, with the camera in front of him. Beside the camera were two screens, one showing the live feed from Ron O'Hara's audience-filled studio, and one on a live feed of Hesson's opponent, filmed at his house in conservative hell, aka California. As expected, O'Hara's opponent was liberal human rights activist Les Vinahee, a UFO (Ugly, Fat, and Old), the standard on ATNN to improve the image of the conservative debater.

Baron's secretary had replaced his gold pen collection with a pencil shredder, and replaced the photos on Baron's back wall from pictures of Baron with pop stars to family photos. The producer in front of him counted down to show time with his fingers. 5, 4, 3, 2, 1, show time.

The studio audience applauded and so the show began.

"Welcome back to the America True News Network," Ronald O'Hara, the channel's anchorman, said. "The one network that..." O'Hara motioned to the crowd.

"Isn't run by greedy liars who hate America!" the crowd chimed in.

Hesson smiled, ATNN's brainwashed crowd provided quite a home field advantage.

"That's right folks, I'm your host Ron O'Hara, and we are in for quite a show today. First off, we have two valued guests in to discuss the latest happenings in Bangladesh. As you know, there was a bit of an incident in Bangladesh over the weekend. A bit of a fire, a few deaths, at a factory whose products supply clothing for companies such Savers Super Mart-"

"A few deaths?" the UFO, Les, scoffed, "stop trying to downplay the atrocious-"

"Shut up! Shut up, you dirty liberal. You can act however you wish when you're on one of your liberal shows, but on my show, on my network, you speak when spoken to and keep your damn mouth shut when others are talking."

Rowdy applause as the UFO was caught in shellshock, a first-timer on O'Hara's show.

"Now please excuse me everyone, but I feel we all have to know our manners, even Leftists."

Laughter.

"Now, back to the show. As I was saying, there was an accident at a Bangladesh plant, on the other side of the world, a few Bangladeshis get hurt, working at a Bangladeshi factory. Now, don't get me wrong, I'm praying for those poor families, but I do not even understand people like you, Les, that blame great American companies like Savers Super Mart."

"Yes Ron. The thing is, American companies such as Savers Super Mart and other American brands contract suppliers from many factories in Bangladesh-"

"Hold it right there, you said those factories are suppliers for Savers Super Mart?"

"Yes, they-"

"So Savers Super Mart does not actually have employees there?"

"No, but-"

"I don't see how this can be Savers Super Mart's fault."

"Because suppliers are under so much pressure to provide cheap labor-"

"They don't have to if they don't want to. Savers Super Mart cannot force these workers into working. And I heard these employees rather appreciate these jobs. Without these jobs they would be homeless and poor."

"Since you brought that up, Ron, the average wage for a factory worker in Bangladesh is $.60 a day, they are still extremely poor. They can't even afford to buy bread for their families-"

"Oh yeah, wise guy? From our survey, it states of the thousands of factory workers in Bangladesh, all of them, as in 100% of them, agree that they are so grateful for the jobs provided from these factories, and they do not blame American companies one bit-"

"Where do you get your stats from? That's ridic-"

"SHUT UP! What did I say about speaking when spoken to?"

"You are lying to the American public-"

"SHUT UP! I have no choice but to mute you!" With the press of a button, the UFO was muted.

"What do you say America? Off with his head?"

"OFF WITH HIS HEAD," chimed the audience.

"So be it," O'Hara grinned. A picture of the UFO during the interview popped up, and a cheap graphic showed his head tumbling off the body. The crowd roared.

O'Hara turned his attention to Hesson. "Now, time to talk to someone with manners... and with a brain—Baron Hesson. Welcome to the program, and sorry for not being able to ask you anything earlier."

"No need to apologize, it's always entertaining to put liberal punks in their place."

Raucous cheering.

"Right you are there, Mr. Hesson. Can we start off by giving this man a round of applause?" The crowd joined O'Hara in a standing ovation for a good 30 seconds before the audience followed O'Hara's lead when he took his seat. "For those of you that don't know, Mr. Hesson is the CEO of Savers Super Mart, the greatest American store of today's time and the official sponsor of our program. Not only do you bring in over a trillion dollars in annual revenue, but you employ 16% of the American population. Thank you."

More applause.

"Please, please. That is not necessary, I do what I do to serve all of you, and to serve America," Hesson forced his most faux-genuine smile, then tried his best Oprah vocal impression. "The greatest country in the world!"

More raucous cheering, followed by a hearty "U-S-A" chant.

"Wonderful, wonderful Mr. Hesson. A true patriot you are. So my next question is, now as we've already determined, Savers Super Mart is not at fault with this accident. It's not your fault. The company is great, yet anti-American liberals keep trying to tear you down."

That wasn't really a question, but Baron knew what to say. "You're right Ron. We have nothing but the highest standards for our employees, whether in America or abroad. We had no hand in this matter. Regardless, we take it upon ourselves to better those around us. That's why I would like to use your show to announce our new organization to reduce incidents like these to make factories around the world a safer place. We call it *Help Eliminate Loss of People*, or *HELP* for short."

O'Hara's face perked up like it was Christmas morning. "Wow! It even has *help* in the title. What a great company."

O'Hara initiated another round of applause as Hesson grinned, a piece of cake.

Day Zero

My job is to sew pockets. Breast pockets onto suit jackets. All day. All night. Every day. Every night. Four breast pockets (two inside and two outside) for each nice suit jacket to be worn at weddings, interviews, dances, fancy occasions. Pockets to hold wallets, credit cards, cell phones, car keys. Things I never will know. Things I will never need. Things I will never want.

I sit in my chair, at my sewing machine, 16 hours a day. Busy with my work, sewing four pockets into 800 suit jackets a day. 3,200 pockets a day, every day.

It's almost 8:00pm. I cannot tell this by my watch, for I have none, nor by the light outside, for we have no windows, but by the number of suit jackets I've completed today, 2,682. When you've been at this as long as I have, you know these things.

I do the same task, day-in day-out. Not for the money. I only make 200 taka a day, barely enough to buy bread for my child and I. I want my daughter to live a life, a real one. One not wasted deteriorating inside a sweatshop. I want my daughter to have dreams and not have to throw them into the wind, as dreams, nothing more than to blow farther away from her 'til she can no longer see them. I want to bury her dreams in the soil, to grow into the largest tree. Substantial and anchored in reality. Because dreams do not come true overnight, they take time and nurturing and faith, knowing that even if you can't see it with your own eyes, you know it's there.

My daughter, Aśā Kari, isn't living her dreams; she's working one floor above me, sewing pants for the same company. She cries more and more, but I tell her to have hope. I made sure she would always have hope on her mind. Her dreams are beneath the ground now, but they will surface when it's time. Aśā Kari may think to lose hope at times but I will never allow it, for she is my hope.

Pain sears my back. "BACK TO WORK! FOCUS!" screams the floor manager. My pace must have eased as I pondered.

I apologize and regain focus and speed up my work to catch up.

"Don't let me catch you slowing down again."

I focus, hard. I forego thoughts of the heat, fatigue, and wariness. This job is far too important. I need this job.

I hear heightened voices in the far side of the room. The heightened voices turn to some screams, then more. I do not dare look up; I cannot risk being caught unfocused again.

The woman next me, I have not learned her name despite working side-by-side for six months, screams "Fire!" I can't resist, I look up to see the colossal flames in the far corner, spreading by the second, already consuming a third of the floor. The fire was about 75 meters away.

"BACK TO WORK! BACK TO WORK! IF I SEE ONE OF YOU NOT WORKING YOU ARE ALL FIRED!"

I try to focus, but three pockets later I can't go on. The fire is 50 meters away, I must do something. I'm on the second floor, my daughter, Aśā Kari, is on the floor above me. She is not yet 10, she has a life to live.

I stand up and almost fall over from exhaustion. I stumble out of my chair, I see the floor manager pacing toward me to beat me with his paddle but as soon as I stand, my entire line stands and runs for the door and their lives.

There's a stampede as we sprint to the doors. Some women are trampled. The doors are locked from the outside. There is no escape. Everything in here is old and dilapidated, but the doors are steel and stern.

I scan the surroundings to find something that can help. I run against the tide of frantic workers to grab a fire extinguisher hanging on the wall, inside its protective metal casing with a glass cover so I can see it's there. The case is locked, so I grab the nearest sewing machine and summon the strength to smash it against the glass case, shattering the whole thing in one try. I snatch the fire extinguisher and pull it from the protective metal casing. All that used to be red and silver is now rust. I can barely see the English wording anymore. I race toward the fire, extinguisher in hand. I stop five feet short of the flames, my skin already burning. I aim the nozzle at the base of the flames and squeeze the lever. Then again. Then again. Nothing comes, not even a drip.

Without hope, or what Bangladeshis refer to as āśā kari. The fire now owns more than half of the floor. The hundreds of us huddle in any temporary shelter we can find. If only we could gather our tears, we could put out these flames.

A snapping sound, and a column fifty yards away, in the middle of the fire crumbles, pulling out the support for the floor above us, and the two floors above that one. As if watching an upside-down sinkhole, the hole above us spreads and spreads our way. All I can do is embrace those around me and kneel to the ground as the world collapses on us. I look down, not in fear, but because I know exactly what will kill me, and I have known for a long time.

O   O   O   O   O   O

Sometime later I regain consciousness but do not regain mobility. I'm pinned underneath three floors of rubble. Above me, just barely, I can see the black of night. I cannot move, just think, and pray that Aśā Kari somehow survived this massacre. If she is still alive she must be so scared. I remember when I was just a girl, like her, I was ten years old when the factory I worked in with my mother caught on fire. I somehow managed to survive but my mother did not. That was the worst day of my life. I remember watching from afar at the mass of broken concrete, and vowing I would find a way so my daughter would never have to grow up in a factory like I did. But I failed. Change never came.

"Aśā Kari! Aśā Kari!" I scream until I can't scream. I will call out for her until I have no more breath in me. I can hear and feel the fire, not too far from me now. I refuse to blink as I stare at the night visible through the smallest of openings above me. I know I will die here but I just want to see one glint of sunlight, one small sign that the new day is coming before I leave. I do not know how long I was unconscious, but I feel the new day is too far away from me now. The fire will rage on until there is no more. The fire is grabbing me now. My story ends here, the story of hundreds and thousands of families will end here in the fire. From the ash rises nothing.

Falling Stars

"Then I'll get whatever $2 can get me, then. Shittttt."

The bartender/pizza artisan/cashier/full-time student stared at Vincent, amused with his desperation. She loved talking to the short, scrawny Asian kid who spoke in flimsy Ebonics and who tried so hard to sound tough, yet could never quite mask the slight—but absolutely detectable—Asian accent. "You know, 4 pm is a little bit early to be needing some alcohol. And I'm pretty sure the thug rappers you're trying to imitate don't drink 21 Club," Anita said, motioning to Vincent's get-up—baggy jeans, oversized t-shirt, and gold-colored plastic necklace.

"I don't need it yo, it helps calm me for performing. I'll be taking the stage in a few minutes."

"Oh yeah?" teased Anita, the big-boned Hispanic who was speaking with the sarcastic tone her heritage was known for.

"What's that supposed to mean? 'Oh yeah'?" Vincent tried to match the bartender's sarcasm, but even when exaggerating, he didn't come close.

"Because you come in every Wednesday for Open Mic Night, you stay for the whole time and never perform. Even when there's no one performing for 30 minutes you never get up there."

"Well I wasn't ready before, I'm ready now."

"Stop lying to yourself, you've been coming here for far too long. If you ever had it in you to perform, it would have been a long time ago."

"Look atchu standing in yo damn glass house. I've never seen you go up there."

"Yeah, you're right. No way would I ever do that. I WORK HERE," the bartender pointed to her name tag. "I'm just here because it's on campus, and every now and then, I actually get a decent tip, but you don't see me going around, bragging about how I'm the next big thing, the 'Asian Eminem.' I don't have a problem with you doing it either, but rapping isn't your thing, it's just a dream. You have plenty of dreams, but you don't have the guts to do nuthin bout it."

Vincent was taken aback.

"Look, I'm only telling you this because we're classmates, I think you're a good guy, and you never tip anyway so I don't really have anything to lose."

"Nah it's ok Shawty, I appreciate it. Gives me fire to write, fire to succeed."

The bartender continued to stare at Vincent, not blinking according to Vincent's account, sighed, and reached below the counter and pulled up a 21 Club Beer can. "This is the cheapest beer we have. I'll give it to you for two bucks."

Vincent winced, grabbing the light, fizzy beer, notorious on college campuses for the high alcoholic content and low cost. 21 Club knew their strengths, too, as their motto was "21 Club: hey, at least it's alcohol." 21 Club was the ideal example of the economic term *inferior cost*: when you starting making any kind of money, your consumption of 21 Club was the first thing to go.

"Hey, I'm doing you a favor, you know. 21 Club is $3."

"But doesn't your register have to balance at the end of the night?"

"Yeah it does, so I'll spot you the extra dollar. Can you believe that? I'm actually paying to serve you."

"No, I can't take this. Gotsta watch my street cred, 'ya hear?"

"What street cred? This is Orange County. More importantly, I'll beat you up if you don't."

Although only semi-serious, Vincent had no question that she could beat him up if she desired—when she wasn't working the night shift at the pub, she was playing women's club rugby.

"Thanks, I won't forget this when I have my first platinum record." Vincent swapped the two dollars for the 21 Club and grabbed his seat near the back of the room. Not a bad showing tonight of about 30 people, filling up about half of the underground pub, and most of them at least partially paying attention to the performer. Vincent couldn't stop thinking about his earlier conversation. Was he a phony?

The 21 Club accomplished its intended mission in delivering a decent buzz. To say 21 Club soothed his pain would be inaccurate. 21 Club was too bitter, harsh, and awful to ever rightfully share a sentence with sooth. However, it's more appropriate to say the beverage diverted his pain, kind of like stubbing your toe and then, in reaction, hitting your head on the wall behind you. The head hit stings just as bad but at least it takes away from the pain of the toe-stubbing. Kinda.

Vincent was half-way through the can, staring into its gold-letters as if it held the secrets to the world. The sounds of the open mic performers blended and blurred. It was the afternoon session, so it was a sober crowd, consisting of friends taking a study break and the serious-minded performing arts majors who came out every week to sing and dance with the hopes of being discovered.

At 4 pm.

On a Wednesday.

At a small college pub.

That's underground.

In a city nowhere near Los Angeles or New York.

Amid the inconsistent vocals and polite applause, one voice stood out to Vincent as he searched for answers in his beer can. The singer's voice was breathy, pitchy and lacked power, but was also pretty, feminine, and calming. He looked up to see her on stage, strumming a sleepy melody on her worn-down acoustic guitar with her eyes closed. The lyrics were familiar. It was neither a current pop-hit, nor a karaoke classic, but very familiar. The lyrics rang as hollow as the singer's voice.

"I still love you, no matter what you do

I still love you, forever these words are true

Every time I see you, it feels like love anew

Who would've ever knew, that with all that you do

My words are still true, I'm in love with you"

And so on and so on. The singer was older, probably late 30s, which possibly meant she was a late bloomer reaching for higher education. But this singer, with her blonde hair in curls, was different. Vincent remembered this song; it was "I Still Love You" by Daisy Green. He remembered his older sister playing it all the time when he was growing up. She played it non-stop whenever she was having boy problems during middle school and high school (WHICH WAS ALL THE FRICKIN' TIME). This particularly posed a problem because they shared a room together. His sister hung Daisy Green posters, full of hearts, flowers, and pink, on her half of the room, causing quite a clash with Vincent's macho posters of the Anaheim Angels (back when they were the Anaheim Angels). Ironically enough, Daisy dated two of the players Vincent had posters of, but that's neither here nor there. With Daisy Green's image ingrained into his memory, it took an instant, if not less, for Vincent to realize it was the real deal performing.

Daisy finished her song (consisting of 10 rounds of "My words are still true, I'm in love with you"), and said "thank you, I'm Daisy Green," in her accent that was equal parts Valley girl and country sweetheart, and was met with polite applause as with everyone else. Daisy relished the minute appreciation and then knelt down to start packing up her guitar. *Did no one realize who she was?* Vincent wondered. Maybe this wasn't so odd after all. Vincent quickly did the math in his head: his sister, who was 6 years older, was really into Daisy Green in the mid-90's, starting in 7th grade, when she was 13, and having her interest die out about four years later, when she was 17. So Vincent, now 24, endured his sister's obsession with Daisy Green when he was ages 5-9, so his college peers, who mostly fall in the 18-21 age range, for the most part missed the brief cataclysmic tidal wave that was Daisy Green. Due to Vincent's late change of career objectives, his time in school extended, leading him to be 3-4 years older than most of his classmates.

With no doubt in his mind, Vincent had to talk to her. He got up, started walking toward the stage when he quickly reversed, placing his half-empty 21 Club (and saying half-empty was thinking on the bright side, with the way 21 Club tasted) back on the table. There was no way

Vincent would be caught by Daisy drinking the cheapest beer. *What was Daisy Green doing here?* As Vincent approached her, he analyzed Daisy, saw how her beauty was still apparent, though she wasn't aging gracefully. Her hair damaged and her eyes baggy. She dressed in the same tight washed-out jeans and tube top she probably performed in during her heyday. Finally, her slight muffin top proved she hadn't altered her diet for her slowing metabolism. As he closed to within 15 feet, his teenage fear struck, regardless of how her body may have deteriorated a bit, but Vincent still could only think of Daisy Green, former teenage worldwide sensation. Vincent may have hated Daisy's music upon his first introduction, but as he grew into his teenage years, his loathing transformed into lust. Daisy, with her golden locks, perfect smile, and innocent yet skin-bearing sun dress occupied Vincent's mind for countless nights. Even after his sister had moved out, Vincent refused to move Daisy Green's poster.

What the hell do I say? He closed within 10 feet, slowing down to create an additional second to come up with something to say, clever or not. For an aspiring rapper, Vincent never excelled at thinking on his feet. 5 feet away, Vincent was drawing a blank, but had to stop because any closer and things would start to get really weird. Daisy looked up from her guitar case, at him, Vincent Lee, who absolutely had nothing to say, zero, nada, zilch. Screw it, it was his time to shine.

"Wh-wh-wh-wh-wh-wh-wha-wha-wha- hi-h-hiii."

O   O   O   O   O   O

"Thank you, I'm Daisy Green," Daisy said, and was met with a mild applause from like 8 people of the 20-person crowd. *Totally embarrassing*, Daisy thought as she moved off the stage and started packing up her guitar. Sixteen years ago today she was mesmerizing a 100,000-person crowd in Europe for her international tour (according to her calendar, which she kept all of her past tour dates); and today, she was tolerated by a handful of students too lazy and anti-social to go outside. After considerable thought, Daisy determined this may very well be one of the worst days of her life. Daisy had to keep pushing, however, because it was only a matter of time before she regained her popularity and went on her massive comeback tour. As long as she was looking this hot in these shredded jeans, she knew she was going to make it back on top.

Daisy strained her ears for any last-minute pleas for an encore, but none came. Daisy figured it was due to a *No Encore* rule or something.

As she finished packing up her guitar, she heard footsteps approach. Daisy looked up to see a scrawny Asian kid, probably 5-15 years younger than her (you can never tell with Asians).

"Wh-wh-wh-wh-wh-wh-wha-wha-wha- hi-h-hiii." the kid said in a noticeable Asian accent, directing Daisy to figuring he was about 15 years younger.

"Hi." Daisy's southern accent masked her irritation with her new visitor.

"Hey, I mean, yo," the boy said, lowering his voice, trying to recover with a cheap thug impression, "I heard you playing up there, I remember listening to that song play on the radio all the time growing up. I'm a, I mean, my sista was all over yo music when she was a child."

"Aww, thanks." Hmmm, the extremely shaky introduction followed by an effort for a more calm approach. Daisy was an expert with this behavior. Over the years thousands of boys, ranging from 13 to 50, approached her, shocked initially with her star power, only to try to save face and try way too hard to come off as the arrogant jerks they had initially aimed to be portrayed as, which Daisy never understood. For the most part these interactions ended with the boy shyly admitting their love, or a half-baked marriage proposal, or a nonchalant mentioning of a future date, as if to convey they could care less about the biggest superstar on the planet's response. Daisy was more than curious to see which box this one would fall into. Previously bored with the endless stream of marriage proposals, topping 300 a day sometimes, Daisy now went a handful of shows at a time without being recognized at all.

"Yeah, as a musical artist myself, it's great to see such a big star come to the middle of nowhere. Maybe we could collaborate on something."

Wow, an artistic collaboration proposal, Daisy wasn't counting on that one. "Oh yeah?"

"Yeah, check this out, you're a big star worldwide, and I'm a pretty big deal around here, so it just makes sense, ya hear?"

"Oh my God, that's totally like a great idea, right?" Daisy was still suspect as to this kid's talent or local fame, but loved how he talked about her fame in the present tense. "But how do I know you're such a big shot?"

"Uh, what?" The tenseness returned to the kid's face right as the tough-guy act departed.

"You said you're a big deal around here."

"Uh, yep. I mean, yo, yeah, fo real."

"And so this is like your home turf then, right?"

"Uh, yeah, yeah, one of many turfs, turves…turfs. Tur-vv—sss?"

"Okay then," Daisy turned to the nearest person, the barkeep, "Excuse me, this man—" she looked back at the Asian kid, "Sorry babe, what's your name?"

"Vincent, I go by Vin-Real, though."

Daisy did a double take and redirected her attention back to the barkeep. "So Vin-Real said he's a big deal around here, he's a big singer and all—"

"Rapper, I'm a rapper."

You gotta be kidding me. An Asian rapper? I guess strange things can happen in the middle of nowhere. "Beg my pardon Sugar," Daisy said, turning her head back to the barkeep, "he's apparently a big rapper around here. Is that like true?"

The barkeep glared, both at Daisy and at Vin-Real, "Oh yeah, he's a big deal alright."

"Wonderful, thank you, Darling." Daisy turned back to the Asian kid, whose relief turned to his cool face, like there was no question in the matter. "Sorry hun, just needed to check that you were telling the truth. I meet a lot of phonies. Know what, to make it up to you I'll buy the next round. You were the one sitting in the back with 21 Club, right?"

"Woah, no no, I don't drink 21 Club, girl please."

"No? WHATEVER!" Daisy formed a W with her two hands. "No, I saw you sitting in the back drinking, no one else was sitting in the back. Don't even lie."

"Oh, Oh! Yeyyyah, my friend was with me, he left before you started performing."

"Oh, okay, that actually like totally makes sense. Good, because I wouldn't be caught dead drinking that stuff." He was obviously lying, Daisy was certain. It's not that it was hard to tell because the presence of a beautiful woman, such as herself, was more effective than any polygraph test at detecting a man's lie. "Darling, a pitcher of beer please, whatever is one level above 21 Club because Vincent doesn't drink 21 Club and neither do I."

Daisy and Vincent sat down at the table in the back that Daisy saw Vincent sitting at earlier. Vincent asked the busboy to clean off the table, being that the 21 Club can didn't belong to him. The busboy looked puzzled but complied when Vincent shot him a *just do it* glare.

"So Daisy, let's be real, I ain't sure whatchu doin round here, performing at a college pub's open mic night and all."

"Well, I'm trying to keep this quiet but—" Daisy leaned in, and didn't resume until Vincent finally did the same, "I've been taking a break, and I'm going to be coming back, do like the biggest world tour of all time. I'm just here to like practice."

"Wow!" Vincent was literally blown back by the news, before remembering Daisy's wish to keep things quiet. Vincent returned to a whisper, "I mean, wow, Daisy Green's gonna be making a comeback."

"AS IF! IT IS SO NOT A COMEBACK!" Daisy checked her voice, returned to a whisper, "It is not a comeback, let's make that clear."

"Chill home girl. But you just said you be coming back."

"Coming back to music and making a comeback are two entirely different things. Comebacks are for past-their-prime divas that no one likes anymore and are attempting to be loved again. Comebacks are SOOO pathetic. I, on the other hand, decided to take a break from music, and will be returning where I left off, on top of the world."

"Oh ok," Vincent didn't believe her, one of many. Daisy took a big gulp. "Although I know my life is interesting and all, I need to take a break. Tell me about yourself. How long have you been doing music for?"

"Well, I'm a student here, was a math major, up until a few semesters ago, decided to switch majors, follow my true passion, music. So I stopped my math program and enrolled in the music production program here."

"Wow, that's pretty drastic. Were you far along in your math program?"

"One semester away."

"And you quit?"

"Well I didn't quit school, just changed majors, yo. It will push back my grad date a couple years, but I'll still get a bachelors, just in music now."

"Wow, math, you must be a smarty pants then."

"I was a'ite."

"Alright? Aren't all Asians good at math?"

"Shizzz, that's racist yo...but yeah."

"Well, what was your GPA?"

"I don't know, I think it was about—" Vincent looked at the ceiling, as if searching for any record of his GPA, Daisy didn't have time for this sudden streak of modesty.

"What was your GPA?"

"3.96."

"Holy cow!"

"It's not that big a deal."

"Uh, yeah it is. You're a genius! You could be making like a ton of money solving math problems, or whatever math majors do."

"I mean, yeah, I could've had a nice living and all that jazz, but it's just not what I wanted. I wanta be a musician."

"Well good for you, following your dream. Becoming a superstar is hard work, Vincent. You know the only thing harder?"

"What?"

"Staying a superstar."

Vincent chuckled, "I have to become a star first, and then I'll bother with the rest."

Daisy looked Vincent in the eye and chuckled.

"What?"

"You know, you're kinda cute when you're not trying to act like a gangster and everything."

Vin-Real immediately became defensive, "Woah now girl, you don't know me. Just cuz I good at math don't mean I didn't grow up tough."

"Easy there tiger. Maybe you should call your doctor to get an extra strong prescription of chill pills," Daisy held her hands up in surrender, mocking and unthreatened, while also giving a hearty laugh at her own joke. Odd that Vincent didn't laugh, that was one of her better ones. It's weird how the jokes she got huge laughs from fifteen years ago she wasn't even getting a smile from today. Daisy wondered why men didn't have the same sense of humor that they used to. "I'm sorry, I don't know all about you. But now I know a little bit about you, I wanna hear some of your stuff."

"Excuse me?"

"I want to hear you rap, Vincent, see how good you really are."

"I don't know, I—"

"Come on Vincent, or should I say Vin-Real? Don't ask me to believe you're a big deal around here and you can't even do an open mic, hit the stage," Daisy motioned to the stage behind her, "It's open, it's SOOO calling your name."

"I mean, I don't even have any of my equipment set up."

"Ah, don't be a sissy. Fine, just do a song right here."

"Here?"

"You heard me, here, I'll give you a beat." Daisy cupped her hands and started a beat, *bfffffff, chck, bf bf bf chk, bfffffff chk, bf bf bf chk*. Daisy's eyes urged Vincent on, especially after 10 seconds.

Vincent froze and with his peripherals could see eyes peering over at their table, hearing her beat boxing from several tables down. Finally, he took the leap.

"You think you cool, think you rule dis

But you just a tool, cuz Vin-Real be the real shit

Don't mess with me, or else I'll guarantee

That you'll swim across the big blue sea

To get away from me

I'm pop you suckers up

Murder all you family

Knock yo girlfriend up

Then when your homies come at me

I'll take my gun out and go

Bang bang bang

If you call the cops on me

I'll load my gun and go

Bang bang bang-

Daisy couldn't contain it anymore, she burst out laughing. "Stop, stop, please stop."

The sudden outburst caught Vincent by surprise, who had crescendoed as the verses progressed. "What? What's wrong?"

"I'm sorry Vincent, but come on, who do you think you are? Some gangsta?"

"What are you talking about?"

"Oh come on, listen to yourself. Guns, murder, popping suckers, that's not you."

"Don't tell me who I am, you don't even know me!"

"Woah, woah, woah," Daisy put her hands up in a mocking fashion, "just don't take your gun out and go bang, bang, bang. I might like totally chip a nail."

"Shut up, how do you know I don't have a gun right now?"

"Uh, because you're some scrawny, 5-foot-tall Asian kid who's a MATH MAJOR at a FOUR-YEAR COLLEGE! I bet you even weigh less than me... so that would mean that you weigh less than 100 pounds," Daisy looked around, and was pleased that no one reacted to her last statement.

"Damn it, shut up! I've had to work for everything I've ever had, okay? You don't think I haven't heard all these criticisms before? Please, no one has ever been on my side. Plus, don't act like you're singing songs about who you really are. I mean you're in your thirties and are still singing songs you wrote when you were fifteen. I mean, even when you came out with new albums, every single song would be about your first love or sending love notes or some shit like that."

"Hey, that is SOOOO unfair. That's because that's the music my fans love. Okay, I play songs like "I Still Love You" every night because my fans love songs like that. I have plenty of other material. You don't even know."

"Prove it."

"I so, like, don't have anything to prove to you."

"I just rapped for you gurl, it's only fair for your turn to be up, ya hear?"

"Fine." Daisy reached down for her guitar case.

"Nuh uh, no need for equipment, just sing."

"Okay, a cappella it is. I'm going to totally rule your world right now."

O   O   O   O   O   O

Shizz man, who is Daisy Green to say I am a phony. Not to say she is wrong, but still. Vincent was still licking his wounds from the bartender's tirade, let alone Daisy's comments. *Shit, fuck everyone, they don't know anything.* Story of Vincent's life.

Daisy closed her eyes and began with her breathy voice in a soft melody:

You try to make everything okay

By asking about my day

And saying you will change

Just like it's still yesterday

But, no, I cannot take you back

Can't pretend it'll be like the past

No, my answer will never change

Because…

Daisy paused as she opened her eyes, as if to give Vincent ample time to eat his words. Which seemed more and more like a possibility. Not a huge stray from her past material, but admittedly a not-completely-insignificant step toward female empowerment. Daisy breathed in and reclosed her eyes.

I don't love you, no matter what you do

I don't love you, forever these words are true

Every time I see you, I feel no love anew

How could you not have knew, that with all that you do

My words are still true; I'm not in love with you

Daisy opened her eyes to the biggest smile she'd ever seen on Vincent, since she met him 20 minutes ago. "So, I guess this means I'll have to accept your apology, then."

"HAHAHA," Vincent said, "That's not original. You just sang "I Still Love You" but added in *don't*."

"No I didn't!"

"Fo sho you did, think about it. Fo realz."

The two were silent for a good 45 seconds as Vincent watched Daisy mouth out the words to the two songs, and then take a pen out from her purse and take another 2 minutes to scribble out the lyrics on a napkin. All those hours Vincent spent gazing at Daisy Green's poster to only now find out that the real thing was not much different than the poster, shiny and beautiful, but lacking any kind of depth.

"Fine, I guess you're right."

"Damn girl, can't believe you just figurin' dat out."

"Shut up! Maybe if you weren't so mean you wouldn't be drinking here alone all the time."

"Maybe if you stopped acting like a fifteen-year-old you could actually write a new song for once!"

No response; time to pounce.

"I mean, come on, how pathetic are you? You talk like you're in high school, you dress like you're in high school; what the hell is wrong with you? You sing like you're a teenager that's never been kissed when you're really a washed-out has-been with no signs of ever growing up."

Daisy and Vincent both jumped to their feet, kicking their chairs behind them. Both had their arms straight and unbent, pressed against the table top, ready to tear each other apart.

"At least I'm not some two-faced jerk who pretends he's *such a big deal*. But deep down, you're all talk, you're too scared to perform for one girl. Yeah right, next big thing. AS. IF."

"Coming from the has-been. Can't get over the fact that the world passed you by and left you for dead. Knowing that you were famous but now no one even gives a damn about you. Because people only listened to Daisy Green when they were too frickin' stupid to know better."

"At least I had a time. Your time will never come because you're too much of a loser to go out there and get it. Maybe I live in the past, but I'm still performing, I'm still trying to live my life, not drink it away with dreams of what I said I wanted to be when I was in kindergarten."

"HEY, ASSHOLES IN THE BACK!"

Vincent and Daisy paused their shouting match to turn and see the person with the microphone was screaming at them. It was "Big" Bertha Pansowinowich. Bertha fell in the category of performing arts majors hoping to catch their big break. This clearly wasn't going to happen for "Big" Bertha, she failed all potential criteria for potential superstar success. In the past, you had to be the best of the best to succeed. "Big" Bertha wasn't even close. But hey, now you don't even have to be talented in the music biz. If you don't have a good voice, just be smokin' hot. Big Bertha failed here too. Just to clarify, her nickname was in no way ironic, and neither was it figurative (*i.e. Big Bertha is a big deal at our campus*). But hey, what about the hilarious fat chick!?! Well, of all the bones Bertha has eaten, either by accident or by sheer laziness, not one of them was a funny one. A classic three-strikes-and-you're-out broad. *God, Bertha's still yelling at us.*

"This is not screaming hour, this is open mic hour! I've waited my turn and listened to you sorry losers! Did I say how much you both sucked? Nooo! I sat patiently and politely to wait for my turn! You two can kill each other for all I care, but not here! Unlike some of you, some of us here are trying to become something, and this is my chance!"

"Shut up, you fat bitch!"

"YOU shut up! I have the fucking microphone, so I'm the only one in here that should be making any noise. You should all be listening to ME! I have a beautiful voice, goddamit! And a heart of gold!"

Vincent could tell how furious Bertha was by how her fat jiggled, it was like an earthquake or something. He saw the bartender, now acting as bouncer, make her way over to Daisy and him.

"Know what? We're out of here."

Daisy and Vincent gathered their few belongings: a purse and a backpack; and made their way out of the pub, finally quelling Bertha's gigantic rage.

"Yeah, you two get out of here, we don't need your kind here." Bertha directed her attention back to the crowd, many of whom were lowering their smartphones, sensing the YouTube-worthy segment was over. "Now I'm sorry I got rudely interrupted, but to make it up to you, I'll start from the top!"

Groans sounded throughout the audience as Bertha reset her iPod and restarted a particularly unsavory rendition of "Teenage Dream." On his way out the door, Vincent looked back to see a dozen eyes watching him go, each wishing they had an out, too.

"Damn, I'm glad we got out of there."

"Totally, right? She's so annoying."

Having consumed a pitcher of beer, they both stumbled their way up the stairs to the 1st floor. They had to shield their eyes against the sun since no natural light got through to the underground pub. For some reason, they emerged from the underground floor not wanting to still rip each other's throats out.

"So, I am, like, totally starving right now. Like, I could seriously eat a whole cow if I wasn't watching my hour glass figure."

"Yeah, fo real."

"What's good around here?"

"Uh, there's a bomb burger joint a couple miles out, it's where students go for late night munchies."

"Mmm, sounds delish. Want me to drive?"

"Nah, it's cool, I'll drive." Vin-Real cringed, his car was sporting a brand-new dent from a fender bender Vincent had sustained earlier that day from a collision with another car, a parked car.

"Hey, what's going on over there?" Daisy pointed to the right toward a big gathering with a few dozen tents up.

"Oh, that's the club fair. It's when the student clubs come out and try to get people to join their lame-ass clubs."

"That's a bummer, seems like it coulda been fun, being with all the people and all."

"Yeah, the clubs here SUCK! They'll try anything to get people to join their sorry-ass clubs. They give away pens, food, whatever, but it never works. Losers."

"Woah, woah, woah, woah. Wait, did you say they give away food? For free?"

"Yeah, I mean, that's how desperate these clubs are."

"That doesn't even matter, it's free!"

"Yeah, you're right." Vin-Real was seriously craving a burger now that he had his mind on it, but also remembered the Marianas Trench that was his wallet in its current state. "Yeah, let's do it."

The newly-formed partners-in-crime zeroed in on their first target: the Mexican American Student Association, who was giving away churros in exchange for signing up for their email list.

"Hola," Vincent greeted, even pronouncing the supposed-to-be-silent H.

The MASA member manning the booth was clearly offended but salvaged the interaction with a smile. "Hola señor y señora."

Vincent was about to continue on with his purposely-offensive Spanish accent but Daisy cut him off.

"Buenos días. ¿Cómo estás bien esta tarde? Tenemos mucha hambre," said Daisy, in perfect form and with a genuine accent.

"Ah muy bíen. Gracías. ¿Quieres un churro?" the member asked, reaching into the heat rack for a churro.

"Ah, si, por favor. Y, un churro para mi amigo, por favor."

"Ehhh," the attendant's smile faded as he looked at Vincent and then back at Daisy, "ahh, si. Okay." The attendant snatched another churro and handed it to Vincent. "¿Es un muchacho de tú? Eres seriosa?"

"Si, es simpático, pero muy estúpido."

They both shared a laugh as the attendant handed over the churro.

"Muchas gracías," Daisy said, entering her contact information onto the club's sign-in sheet. As she finished she looked up to the attendant, "*adiós*, buenos días."

"Buenos días."

Daisy departed from the booth and Vincent followed suit.

"What's so funny? Were you laughing at me?"

"Vincent, don't be so paranoid."

"But you both were looking right at me as you were laughing."

"Oh Vincent, you wish. Get over it."

"Fine, then what the hell was that?"

"What?"

"How are you fluent in Spanish?"

"Oh, it's because I speak Spanish."

"I know, but why? Are your parents Mexican or something?"

"No, but my maid was, and I spent like way more time with her than with my parents growing up."

"Oh," Vincent smirked, thinking it was a joke, or at the very least an exaggeration. Then their eyes connected and he saw the depth behind it. "Oh, sorry."

"It's ok." They walked a few strides in an unchallenged silence.

"There's so many clubs out here," Daisy observed, as they walked through the heart of the club fair, with over 100 clubs all around them. "It seems like they have everything here: writing clubs, sports clubs, even, wait, what's that?" Daisy pointed off to her left, straight to a booth offering turkey legs.

Vin-Real smiled, "That's the Zombie-Human Alliance."

"What?"

"Yeah, funny right? These guys are the biggest nerds on campus, let's go talk to them."

"Eww, no!" Daisy scrunched her face as she scanned the booth, seeing only one club member present at the time. "I can't stand nerds, and they all have pizza face."

"But they're giving away turkey legs," Vin-Real teased.

"Uh."

"Sorry, you don't have a choice," Vin-Real utilizing his left arm to tug Daisy's arm, pulling her toward the booth, and using his right arm to catch the attention of the person manning the booth. "Hi-lo there, good sir."

The sole student behind the booth, who was overweight and still thought mullets were "in," shot a look backwards, believing Vincent to be talking to someone behind him, then looked back to Vincent, realizing that he was the one being talked to. "Why good afternoon to you, my good man." The member was overjoyed, despite the promise of free turkey legs, not a soul had visited the booth all day. He snorted with joy.

"Oh and don't mention your real name around these losers, they're all tech geeks so they can track you down," Vin-Real whispered to Daisy right before they arrived at the booth.

"So Zombie-Human Alliance, huh?"

"Precisely! ZHA for short, but call it what you like. Would you like turkey legs? I made them myself."

"Oh, fo sho," Vin-Real said as Spencer forked over two massive barbequed turkey legs. "You a member of this fine establishment?"

"Yessiree, Bob. I'm actually the president, as well as the vice president, treasurer, secretary, and vice president of marketing."

"Oh, wow, why do you have so many titles?"

"Well technically, I'm the only member of the club."

"And what do you mean by technically, yo?"

"Well, I guess I'm just the only member, just sounds better to say technically sometimes," Spencer let out a prolonged chuckle.

Both Daisy and Vincent laughed as well. This newfound camaraderie triggered Spencer's chuckle to develop into a full guttural laugh, and then led to him laughing so loud that it seemed like he was screaming. Eventually his laughs and snorts resided and the conversation resumed.

"So Spence," Daisy said, flashing her big blue eyes at Spencer, "You don't mind if I call you Spence, do you?"

"N-n-no, not at, not at, not at all." No girl had ever spoken this much with him before, excluding his mother, of course.

"Good, so Spence, tell me why are you the only member? I'd think that with all these zombie movies and TV shows, a lot of people would want to join to fight zombies—"

"Now, I'm going to stop you there, I'm sorry, I'm gonna have to stop you there," Spencer voiced his defiance. "Do NOT confuse the ZHA with the Zombie Apocalyptic Fight Club! There IS a BIGGG difference," Spencer insisted.

"Oh?"

"Yes. The Zombie Apocalyptic Fight Club believes that we must kill all the zombies to survive. That's where all the fight practice happens. My club, Zombie Human Alliance, believes that we need to work with zombies and work on not just coexisting, but building a community together," Spence slowed his breathing and softened his voice for dramatic effect. "Just because zombies are the undead, doesn't mean they're not human, too."

Vincent glanced at Daisy. They were both quivering at the lips but restrained themselves from laughter, for now anyways. "Ah I see, so does this Zombie Apocalyptic Fight Club have one member as well?"

"No," Spencer looked down at his feet. "They have eight."

"Oh God," Daisy said, neither Vincent nor her were even trying to play it cool. "You're like not even the most popular zombie club on campus! Among losers, you're the biggest dweeb."

"You don't think I know that? Huh? You know I may not be popular but I'm not stupid, OK? If you're here just to make fun of me, then please just go, and let me be."

"I'm sorry, we're sorry," Vincent said while still laughing. "When's your next meeting practice?"

"Our club doesn't have practices, we have talking sessions, but the next one is tonight from 8-10 pm."

"Okay, and where will that be?"

"The lawn outside the gym."

"Okay, then we'll have to be sure that we aren't anywhere near there at 8 pm tonight." Vincent and Daisy put their heads back and laughed as they walked off into the distance with their Viking-sized turkey legs.

Daisy turned her head back. "Hey, can I get your number, babe?"

"W-w-why do you want my number?"

"So I can put it in my phone blocker, loser!" Daisy turned back to Vincent and they laughed as they resumed their stroll into the distance. Daisy and Vincent were both extremely pleased with their most recent verbal encounter.

"Excuse me," a man's voice called to the left of the partners in crime.

Daisy's eyes became immediately plastered to the man, who was tall, dark and handsome; and also looked 10 years her junior. "My, oh my, hello handsome. What can I do for 'ya?"

The man blushed. "I was wondering if you two were interested in enrolling in some extended education classes over the summer."

"Sorry dawg, that ain't our speed," Vincent declared, "Come on Daisy, let's move on."

"Hey now, hold on, let's hear what this fine young man - I mean fine older gentleman has to say," Daisy resisted. "Go on baby, what are these extended education classes? B-T-dubs, I love your big blue eyes, they remind me a little bit of how big and blue mine are."

The man now was becoming more irritated with Daisy's unsolicited advances. He now crossed his arms to make his wedding ring clearly visible. "Well, it's just a great opportunity to really further your education. We have classes all year-round. And, classes are offered in every subject, whether you need to take some of your core courses, or if you want to learn something completely new."

"OMG that's so great!" Daisy struggled to understand why she couldn't detect any interest from the man at the booth. Now she took out the big guns; batting her eyelashes and twirling her hair through her fingertips. "So I'm like totally interested. Can I get your number so maybe we can talk about this more? Maybe like over dinner or something."

"Here," the man forced his flyer into Daisy's hands. "Here's the list of extended education classes for the summer. IF you have any questions, you may call the number at the bottom to reach the Extended Education Office."

"WHATEVER!" Daisy whined. She crumpled up the flyer and threw it into the man's chest. "How dense are you? I wanted your number so we could go out or something. I don't need to take extra classes. Trying to talk with you is pointless. Ugh."

Now, it was Daisy's turn to pull Vincent by the arm, out of the current situation.

As they escaped, the man yelled "Don't worry, there are flyers everywhere on campus."

"You know, I think this will like be totally enough food for me. Gotta watch my figure, y'know?" Daisy motioned to her muffin top, "They don't call me *Abdominals Daisy* for nothing."

Daisy's antics and speech patterns annoyed Vincent, but he couldn't help seeing Daisy as the teenage superstar that she once was. As unbearable as Vincent found the real Daisy Green, his past perceptions of her kept blocking his view of reality. As a teenager, Vincent longed to be the boy mentioned in Daisy's collection of young-love songs. He yearned to be the boy to show Daisy that not all boys are jerks that break her heart. After all of those years of fantasizing about her, Vincent was not yet ready to let her go. "Yeah that's cool, I think I know a place to sit."

As Vincent guided her to his favorite quiet place, another voice called from his right.

Daisy tugged at his arm, "I think someone is calling you."

"Hey Vincent, Vincent Lee!"

Vincent peered right to see the Mathematical Superstar Club and people he knew very well. Now though, he couldn't be caught being associated with the geekiest group of all. "No I don't know them fools, lessgo."

"LOL, they totally are calling your name, should we go and say hello?" Daisy started pulling him in the direction of the Mathematical Superstar Club's booth.

"NO!" Vincent pulled Daisy off her trajectory as firmly as he spoke, and resumed guiding her to his original destination.

O   O   O   O   O   O

Vincent took Daisy to the top of Humanities Hall, the tallest building on campus. By way of the fire escape they made it onto the rooftop. They devoured their free feast within a couple minutes and were left to stare down at the Club Fair stragglers, and the various booths that were shutting down for the day.

"Sooooooo, what was up with you earlier?"

"Whuz you talkin' bout?"

"Don't be such a silly billy. You were so totally spazzing out to get away from the math group back there. SOOO OBVI."

"I wasn't avoiding them, and it's the Mathematical Superstar Club, to be exact."

"You so were! Do they always take your lunch money or something?"

"Shit, girl? Whatchu been smoking?"

"I'm just calling it like I see it, darling, and you were more scared than a mouse in a snake cage."

Vincent sighed, "I used to be part of them."

"Seriously?"

"Yo, that's the past, shut up, a'ite?"

"Okay, calm down. So what did you guys do all day? Talk about math?"

"Nah, shit! WE did competitions and shit, yo. It was gangsta shit, ya' hear? And when we competed against our rivals, it got real, dawg. It was straight up intense."

"Oh I'm sure, it sounds intense! What was the main injury, stubbing your finger from hitting your calculator too hard?"

"God damn, girl. I swear, if I wasn't a gentleman, I'd be beatin' yo ass."

"Oh yeah," Daisy asked, without the hint of consequence, "like how the jocks beat y'all when they found out where your competitions were held?"

"Whatever, I ain't gotsta put up wid this crap," Vin-Real turned away.

"Okay, okay," Daisy said, for the first time without a hint of mockery. "Honestly though, I mean you were great at math right? Don't you like math?"

"Yeah, I guess so."

"I mean, you like totally could've gotten a great job, a ton of pay, doing a job you love. Why aren't ya doing math then?"

"Are you even aware of the Asian stereotype?"

"What?"

"Ok, if you were to close your eyes, and I asked you what comes to mind when I say Asian, what do you think of?"

"Umm, well I guess I'd say Asians play a lot of video games, are really good at math, really bad at driving, nerdy, and can't speak English."

"Guess what, I was all of those things, all of those."

"Shut up! Seriously?"

"Yeah, seriously."

"But you barely even have an accent anymore. I never would've guessed that you weren't born here in America."

"I was born here, that's why it's so messed up. My parents came here from South Korea before I was born, and they never let me out of the house, so I grew up learning English from them, and they didn't even know how to speak English either. Did you know how bad that sucked in kindergarten when my teacher kept trying to place me in the English as a Second Language class and didn't believe me when I said I was born in California?"

Daisy searched a while for a silver lining. "At least you're good at karate then, right? Like Mr. Miyagi."

"Wow, do you know how offensive that is? Both karate and Mr. Miyagi are JAPANESE. I am KOREAN! Our countries HATE each other! And regardless, I'm not even good at karate. The one stereotype you said that wasn't lame I can't even do!"

"So what, I mean, who cares if you are a living stereotype? Why does that even matter?"
"Iono," Vincent looked down below, "it's like people see me for the first time and they think they know all about me, and sometimes it feels like they're exactly right."

"No joke, I seriously know how you feel. Look at me, I'm blonde, hot, fun. I'm the blonde stereotype."

"You don't even know. You had everything."

"YOU don't even know," Daisy said, spitting Vincent's accusation back at him. I had NOTHING. When I grew up, I dreamed of being an astronaut. I grew up writing and singing about space and how incredible the universe is, and constellations and stuff, but as soon as I got discovered when I was 13, all the producers ever let me sing was about boys and breaking-up. Even when I got older I had to act like I was some simple innocent little girl."

"I never knew that. I thought you were some country girl that lived on a farm."

"No, I grew up in LA. But with all the sexy singers during my time, the label figured I would be much more successful if I came off as some wholesome sweetheart."

"But your accent-"

"A year of voice lessons, that's all that is. After so many years, though, I like can't figure out how to turn it off. I like seriously don't even remember what I used to talk like."

"Then if you hate all this, then why do you still do it? You don't even belong to a label or have a record deal anymore. Why act like you're still trying to please some producer?"

Daisy inhaled a soulful breath. "The longer it all went on, the more committed I got to my new identity, I guess. Like with my voice, I seriously couldn't even find my way back to who I really am." Daisy smiled as tears welled up in her eyes. "You know when I got discovered at 13, I thought that was the beginning of my life. It turns out that it was the end of it. I haven't been myself for so long, I just, I just think sometimes I'll never find myself again."

Daisy looked up in the sky, searching for the answers to questions she's asked herself fruitlessly for years. Vincent reached his hand over to console her.

"HEY, YOU TWO DON'T BELONG UP HERE," said the janitor, who had just appeared from the private access stairway behind them.

Daisy and Vincent must have been talking louder than they thought.

O   O   O   O   O   O

After being kicked out of their luxurious view from above, Daisy and Vincent shared a soundless walk through the quad, which inexplicably led them back to the pub and a pitcher of 21 Club, which they downed in a minute. The highly unadvised amount of cheap beer made them both sick and led them to make trips to their respective bathrooms. After, they returned to their table and ordered another pitcher.

They remained silent and without eye contact until the announcement was made that it was last call for the open mic.

The announcement sent a buzzing through both of their ears as they stared into the empty pitcher and awaited the new one. Neither reacted until Vin-Real broke his stare and looked to Daisy.

"Yo, we should do it."

"Hmm?"

"Let's get up there, let's perform."

"Are you kidding? After all we've talked about? I never want to sing again, ever. Enough is enough. I'm done being a teenage sweetheart and you're done being a wannabe gangster."

"I know, but I'm saying we get up there as you, a past-her-prime diva; and me, an Asian that proves every stereotype in the book."

"No one wants to hear that," Daisy said with the highest sense of detachment. Her eyes staid fixed upon the empty pitcher.

"So what? We've been doing things our whole life to live up to the image set for us by other people. Let's do this for ourselves."

"Like, what are we even going to do?"

"You sing and play guitar, I'll rap along."

"We've never even worked together. There's nothing for us to perform."

"We'll freestyle then," Vincent persuaded.

"But we have 10 minutes, we don't have anything prepared. It will never work." Daisy still hadn't made eye contact with Vincent. Daisy finally looked up, giving Vincent the slightest bit of hope. "Since I turned 13, I've only sung songs written by other people. I can't do this."

"Well I've never performed in front of anyone, we're in this together."

Vincent stood up and held out his hand. Daisy confirmed right then he wouldn't take no for an answer. She took his hand.

The duo arrived on stage just as Anita was about to start unplugging all of the electronics.

"Hey Anita, we're going to perform."

Anita looked at them both, "Well look at that, the great Vin-Real is finally going to perform. Are you sure you don't want to wait until tomorrow? Or even next week?"

"Positive."

"Okay, it's either now or never kids, we're closing down in less than 10."

"Alright," Vincent grabbed the microphone to buy some time for Daisy to set up her guitar. "Hey I'm Vincent Lee and this is Daisy Green. This is our first song together so bear with us."

Daisy's fingers twitched and shook as she struggled to unlock her case. Finally succeeding, Daisy lifted her guitar out of her case and slung it over her shoulder. They looked at each other, and nodded. They faced no jeering from the audience, but that was more due to indifference than patience.

Daisy began strumming a slow melodic tune. She kept strumming for 25, 30, 45 seconds. The dozen or so students left in the pub were becoming antsy. Finally, Daisy sang with her eyes closed; little more than a loud whisper. Her voice as shaky as her hand.

For my whole life, I've never lived

A single day like people thought I did

Thought I was just a girl in a small town

Wearing make-up and winning pageant crowns

Just a skinny girl with blonde hair

A pretty face with a blank stare

All the people think I'm just beautiful

But I know that I've got more to show

Daisy opened her eyes to a nodding crowd. Not a crowd shocked by the sudden change of lyrics or disappointed by her going against the formula, but a crowd enjoying HER music. Daisy had never felt so vulnerable, but this small sign of support gave her the push to truly express herself. She resumed playing, with her voice louder now and her eyes wide open.

And you don't know who I am

You will never understand

You can talk, you can mock

But don't even think that...

You can judge this book by its cover

Because this book isn't nothin' like its cover.

Daisy nodded her head in Vincent's direction, urging him to begin. With his right hand barely managing to grip the microphone,

Vincent took a deep breath and jumped in as Daisy increased the pace of her strumming.

I'm Vincent, y'all don't even think I'm worth 2 cents

You think I'm stupid, think I'm lame, think I'm useless.

Guess what, all the haters in the universe

Can listen on in to the next few verses

Vincent scanned the audience and reaped encouragement from the head-bobbing crowd and the occasional thumbs up.

I used to be a poser

Trying to be cool

Dropping out of school

And acting like a tool

But I learned from my mistake

And will do anything to take

It back, just like that

Resume down my rightful path

Yeah, I'll get back to math

But it aint math that defines me

Now I'll channel my wrath

Not follow false dreams that are shiny

From acting to knowing

Who I am,

Not who I want to become

To act as someone is to become no one

Daisy, hit it.

The crowd cheered as they got onto their feet, excited by the rawness and purity of the performance as Daisy started singing.

No you don't know who I am

Never could you understand

What I've been through

What I've come to

All to stand up and defy you

So before you shut me out

Shut up and hear me now

Don't judge this book by its cover

Cuz this book ain't nothin' like its cover.

As if they had years of experience performing together, Vince sensed it was his time to lay down his last verse.

Yeah you hear that

Like the sun I may always fall

But I always rise again

Then I'll pound you back into the sand

Without unclenching my hand

Without worry of being banned

Have you even heard of Ayn Rand

Happiness is decided by the individual

Without a residual

Of self-doubt or your hatred

While I stand here elated

So go ahead and live your lives politely

Secretly hoping that you were more LIKE ME.

Vincent dropped the microphone, panting and exhilarated. The response from the audience was as boisterous as a 12-person audience could be. No one stayed in their chairs as they applauded with vigor.

O   O   O   O   O   O

Vincent and Daisy held hands as they left the pub for the last time, grinning from ear to ear.

"You know Vincent, you really can rap. Maybe you should stay in the music program," Daisy said, without a trace of her Country/Valley accent.

"No, I'm going to re-enroll in my math program, and finish up."

"Honestly though, you are really good."

"Thanks Daisy. I think I just wanted to prove to myself that I could do this. Plus, I can always do music on the side. Too bad you'll be moving off to a new city and your world tour and everything."

"I think I may have to put off my tour for just a bit longer as well," Daisy said, as she stopped to pluck an extended education flyer off the bulletin board as they passed by.

Daisy and Vincent walked up the stairs and in the dark could make out the outline of an overweight student, Spencer, sitting alone at the lunch tables.

"Poor Spencer," Daisy pouted, "sitting all alone. We were real jerks to him earlier."

"I know, that was the old us though," Vincent said.

"Then the new us should go over and apologize to him."

"That would be too awkward. He probably doesn't want to talk to us."

Daisy immediately stopped in her tracks. "He doesn't want to talk to the old us."

Vincent could tell that Daisy wasn't going to budge. They both walked over to Spencer.

It took a while, but Daisy and Vincent eventually convinced Spencer that they had changed, they would never make fun of him again, and they really were interested in learning. Spencer's speculation dissolved after a while and he unleashed a full education on zombie negotiation 101. Spencer taught them everything from social misconceptions, *zombies do have a sense of humor and sarcasm*; to common courtesies, *ample clothing should be worn at all times around zombies to help them avoid temptation*. After a full two hours, the three parted ways after agreeing to meet the following week, a promise Daisy and Vincent planned to keep.

There was a chill in the air. Vincent and Daisy put their arms around each other. Both figured they were walking each other home, until they realized they lived in the same apartment complex, just a few doors from each other. They were no different; they lived alone in apartments filled with things you could buy at any retail store. Daisy's bedroom was filled with pink and glitter and resembled a teenage girl's bedroom. They agreed to help each other throw everything out the next day.

Later that night, they kissed for the first time. For Daisy, it felt like her first kiss. They kissed several more times that night, all the while Daisy looked over her shoulder as if to make sure her parents weren't about to walk through the front door yelling at her to get her homework done.

All Grown-Ups

"Honey, I'm home."

I exhale a sigh of relief as I wipe my shoes on the doormat and walk into the kitchen.

"Welcome home, darling," my wife, Annie, says with a big smile on her face. She is sitting at our dining room table. She stands up from her plastic chair and approaches me with open arms.

We come close, and move in to kiss, but we don't, cuz that's gross and I don't want all the other boys saying I have cooties or something. But I love Annie and I'm going to marry her someday. Don't tell anyone I told you that, either!

"How was your day sweetie?"

"Long," I replied, mimicking Daddy's response to Mommy every day. I don't get what that means, isn't the day just as long for all of us? Daddy says work is hard, I think work is fun, at least a lot more fun than kindergarten. Daddy gets to drive to work every day, where all his friends are, and play on the computer all day long. THEN, he gets to have lunch with his friends and go wherever they want for lunch. If I could go anywhere for lunch, I would go to McDonalds. Every day. Daddy says he doesn't go to McDonalds, and he eats at food places that don't even sell toys!

"Well you just relax, and sit down, dinner's ready," Annie says as she pulls out my chair for me.

Even as I sit down, I am salivating with anticipation of the main course.

"Mmm, mmm, mmm!" I rub my tummy and lick my lips.

Annie opens up the oven, fanning away the invisible waves of heat with her baking glove. Then, she puts on her baking gloves and reaches into the oven to pull out a yummy plastic cherry pie. It looks just as perfect as it always does. It may not taste very good—I still have a bad taste in my mouth from when I tried to take a bite—but it always looks perfect.

"Mmm, cherry pie, my favorite!"

I don't really like cherry pie, really don't like cherries in general; but it made Annie happy, and that made me happy. So I pretended to take a big bite, secretly pretending it was a chocolate cake, and chewed with my mouth closed, because Mommy says it's rude to chew with your mouth open. I rubbed my belly again, "Mmmm."

She giggles, and now I'm giggling. Maybe I should be a comedian when I grow up. It's noisy all around us, 20 other kids playing during our indoor play-time. We're even louder on days like today when we have a substitute teacher. Our real teacher, Mrs. Mercado, is always mean and grumpy, but substitute teachers always let us play and talk. Mrs. Lightenbooth, today's sub, is really funny because she's really old and can barely hear anything so we have to scream for her to hear us.

Eager to make Annie laugh again, I tried to sound as serious as my father does when I said, "KIDS, quiet down, we're trying to have dinner over here!"

Annie giggles even louder now. Yep, can't wait to go home and tell Mommy and Daddy I'm going to be a comedian when I grow up. I may not be as funny as Mrs. Lightenbooth, but I sure am funnier than Adam Sandler. I've watched all of his movies, even the PG-13 ones, and all you have to do is talk in a funny voice and dress like a girl, sometimes.

Now the whole class starts giggling. Wow, could they all hear me? Now, as I turn my head, I hear the whispers throughout the classroom, "The teacher is sleeping."

There Mrs. Lightenbooth was, sitting behind Mrs. Mercado's desk, fast asleep and mouth wide open.

Andrew, the class troublemaker, stood up from his railroad tracks, and said in a piercing whisper, "Hey, we can play outside!"

Recess was at 11:30, and it was only 10:45, according to my Buzz Lightyear watch. 10:45 is counting practice time, not playtime. Yet one by one, all my classmates followed Andrew's lead and snuck outside, careful to not wake up Mrs. L. After a second, even the teacher's pet, Judy Chan, realized that play was a lot more fun than counting. Soon, it was only Annie and I that were left in the classroom.

"It is a lovely day for tea my darling, don't you say?" Annie asked. She stood from her seat and offered me her hand.

I've never broken a rule before, and I didn't want to start now. Playing outside when it's not your turn is against the rules. If we are caught, I'm pretty sure I'd get detention. I'm pretty sure if I got detention, I'd go to jail for 5 years. Then, if my parents found out I went to jail, I'm pretty sure I'd get grounded and have my video games taken away.

But now, all I wanted was to be with Annie.

"Perfect day, my dear," I said, taking her hand as I stood up. Next to our dining table was a tray with a tea kettle and two cups. I picked it up and walked outside with Annie. We sat down at the shaded table right outside our class door. Annie brought her Princess water bottle with her and poured some water into the tea pot, which I then poured into the two plastic tea cups.

Our tea is nice and cold, which is good because it is really hot outside. Mommy and Daddy say I should play outside more, but I like sitting and watching. Playing games are for kids, drinking tea is for grown-ups. My whole class wanted to be grown-ups already.

In the middle of our playground is a foursquare court and a hopscotch court, but no one ever played on them. We're too busy practicing being adults. It's June, and the school year is almost over. None of us can wait because we are already bored with kindergarten and you get to be more grown-up in first grade.

Everyone is ready to move on and stop being little kids. Ginnie is over on the swings because it's part of her astronaut training. She can go so high that the swing swings almost all the way around. She goes so high that if she let go, I bet she would go straight into space.

Nicholas is right next to the swings, throwing his baseball against the handball wall. He throws against the handball wall because he throws too fast for anyone to catch. He can throw it 100 miles an hour, that's faster than the pros, and I've seen him throw that fast with my own eyes!

Sitting down at the lunch tables is Vessia, she's practicing her speech for the summer school student committee. We all know Vessia's going to win. She's already memorized her speech (a whole 30 seconds!) and she's the class president this year, too. She wants to become the first female president, of either America or the world, and she can count on my vote.

Denny is over by the slide, showing off his brand-new smartphone to the other kids. He wants to become the next Steve Jobs, and he said he already has really cool inventions; but he never tells me what they are, no matter how much I beg, because he says he has to get a patent lawyer first.

"What is going on here?!?" an all-too-familiar harsh adult voice screamed from the handball courts.

Oh no, it's Mrs. C, the playground supervisor. We were all shocked and frozen with fear. Mrs. C lives to hand out detentions to students during recess and lunchtime. Andrew says that she can sense the smallest bit of joy and sets out to destroy it.

"Where is your teacher?"

No one said anything.

"I'll ask one more time, where…is…your…teacher?" she repeats, yelling even louder this time.

I gulped, "Sh-she's inside, sleeping."

"Oh, and you all decided to sneak outside and play?" Mrs. C yelled. "You all should be ashamed of yourselves, taking advantage of poor old Mrs. Lightenbooth! Everyone take a seat at the lunch table and put your heads down. You all are in enough trouble already, but if I hear one word out of any of you or see one of you do as much as move a finger, I will give you two detentions instead of one!"

We all did as she said. Not even Andrew had anything smart to say. We all had our heads down as we shuffled our feet to the red lunch tables and sat down, and put our heads down in our crossed arms. The only sound I could hear was Mrs. C's footsteps walking around our lunch table.

"Now I'm going to go inside, wake Mrs. Lightenbooth up, and when she comes out here, you all are going to apologize to her before I let you go inside. Is this understood?"

Silence.

"Is this understood?"

"Yes, Mrs. C," we all said, together.

I could hear Mrs. C's footsteps walking inside our classroom. I start crying because I don't want to get in trouble. I've never been benched before, or given after-school detention. I try not to cry, because I don't want the other boys to call me a baby; but I can't stop myself. I try to remember my prayers so I can pray the other boys can't hear me. I've never received a detention all year long. I don't know what I'm going to tell my parents. They're going to be so mad. I shouldn't have gone outside to play, I knew it was wrong. Stupid! Stupid! I should have stayed inside. What am I going to tell Mommy and Daddy? My life is over!

We've been waiting for a few minutes and Mrs. C still hasn't come out yet. At least it feels like it's been a while, I don't dare to check my Buzz Lightyear watch, because I don't want Mrs. C to catch me moving.

Finally I hear footsteps coming out to the lunch tables. I can tell more than one person is walking out, Mrs. Lightenbooth must have just woken up.

"Kids, you can sit up now," Mrs. C said, except she didn't sound as angry this time. She sounded quiet and nervous, two things Mrs. C never sounded like. I looked up and saw Mrs. C and Ms. Rayhan, the kindergarten aid. They both looked like they were sick. "Mrs. Lightenbooth is not feeling well, so we're going to have to end class for today. Everyone follow me, we are going to daycare. Once we walk over to the daycare, Ms. Rayhan and I will call all of your parents to come pick you up."

Ginnie raised her hand, "Mrs. C, what about our backpacks?"

"I'm sorry kids, you cannot go back into the classroom right now. We will make sure to keep all of your backpacks and materials safe until tomorrow. Please everyone follow me, we will pick up all your toys as well and bring them inside later. Now form a single file line and no talking, please."

As I get in line behind Annie, I remember something I left in my backpack, my blanket. My blue blanket has been with me everywhere since I've been a baby. I've had it since I was born. Even though I'm almost a first grader, I still feel safe when I'm with my blue blanket. I raise my hand to get Mrs. C's attention.

"Yes?"

"Can I please go back? I really need to get my backpack; I'll be fast, I promise."

"The answer's no."

"But it's really important! I need it!"

Mrs. C sighed. "And why do you need your backpack?"

Now I was at a loss for words. If I said I needed my blanket, I would be made fun of by all the other kids, forever. For the whole year, I hid my blanket at the bottom of my backpack; beneath my lunch pail, folders, and homework. "I can't tell you."

"Well in that case, get back in line."

I did as Mrs. C said and got back in line, head down.

Mrs. C looked away from me when she talked to the whole class. "I'm sorry kids, I know you all want to get your backpacks; but your teacher is very ill. We'll keep your stuff safe, I promise."

During our long walk to daycare, I see an ambulance drive into our school and park next to the curb closest to our class. Kids in my class stop to see where the ambulance is going, but Mrs. C demands that we keep walking, and that we don't look around. Mrs. Lightenbooth must be really sick. I hope she's okay.

In daycare, some of the kids are whispering about what happened. Some kids are saying that she's dead, but I don't believe them. She was fine: she read roll call, she read us a story, and she led us through the Pledge of Allegiance. She was just napping.

After a few minutes, everyone resumed what they were doing before: Vessia practiced her speech, Denny examined his smartphone, and Nicholas made arm circles to keep his joints warm. Yet all the actions were muted: the speech quieter, the concentration less intense, and the arm flailing less rampant. Annie and I walk to the back of the room to pick out a book to read. We walk right past the kindergarten-level books and go straight to the big-kid books. I choose *The Adventures of Barton the Dog*, which is meant for 2nd graders! It only has 5 pictures, too!

After just a few minutes, I am almost done with the whole book (a whole 32 pages!) when Mrs. C taps me on the shoulder.

"Your mom is here to pick you up."

We live really close by, so my mom was the first mom to come. I stand up to pick up my backpack before I remember that everything is still in my classroom. I walk outside and see Mommy right outside the portable building, looking sad, yet, smiling at the same time.

"Billy," she says, opening up her arms wide.

I run to into her arms and give her a big hug. She hugs me just as hard. We start walking home, holding hands. I constantly look around to make sure no one else can see me holding hands with my mommy. Mommy is holding my hand really tight, as if she wants to save me from falling off a cliff.

"Are you okay, my baby?"

"Why are you calling me your baby, Mommy?" Mommy hasn't called me a baby since I was little. Once again, I look around to see if anyone heard her call me a baby. No one did.

"Because you are my baby. You always will be. Are you okay, my baby?"

"Yes, Mommy."

For the rest of the walk I try to ask Mommy a question, but I'm too scared to ask.

"Yes, baby?" Mommy says, looking down at me.

"Nothing, Mommy." I look down so she can't see my face.

"What do you want to say?"

I can't hold it in any longer. "Mrs. Lightenbooth is going to be okay, right?"

Mommy doesn't say anything for a long time, "Mrs. Lightenbooth is in a better place." I can tell she's trying not to cry.

"If she's in a better place then why are you so sad?"

Suddenly, she steps in front of me and kneels down, so she is looking me right in the eyes. She starts crying. "She's in Heaven now, baby."

"So she's, she's, dead?" I stumbled through the sentence, feeling sick as I said the last word.

Mommy paused again, and looked me in the eye. She opened her mouth to speak but no words came out.

"No, she's not! She was fine when class started, she was okay." Now I start crying. I don't even bother trying to hold back the tears.

"It's okay, baby, it's okay. Everything will be alright."

"But how can it be OK if she's not coming back. That's not OK."

"It's just a part of life, my baby."

"What do you mean it's just a part of life?"

"It's okay, my baby."

"But I don't want to die."

"It's okay, baby." Mommy picks me up and cradles me in her arms for the rest of the way home. I press my eyes against her sleeve to stop crying but I can't. I want my blanket.

O   O   O   O   O   O

When class started the next day, Mrs. Mercado and the principal greeted us outside of the classroom. They both said a few words about Mrs. Lightenbooth; about how she lived a long, happy life, and will be remembered for a long time to come. After the principal left, we were let inside the classroom. Everything was left just as it was before: toys lying everywhere and our backpacks hanging on the back of our seats. I ran to my seat to check my backpack. I made sure no one was looking at me before I unzipped it. As I peered inside, I saw my folders, my homework, and lunch box; but no blanket. I searched three more times, each time more frantically than before, but couldn't find it. I started searching a fourth time, but Mrs. Mercado called everyone to gather and sit in front of the whiteboard for roll call.

From that point, class went on as usual. We had story time, counting practice, and show-and-tell presentations. At recess, everyone got in line to play foursquare and hopscotch because no one wanted to play grown-up today.

Black Friday Eve: A True-Life Account of the Legendary Pat Macy with Historical Annotations for Young Readers

200 push-ups, 500 sit-ups, and 5 miles into the daily workout, and Ralph Macy was definitely feeling the burn. Chest heaving, sweat pouring, and calves cramping, Ralph's motivation alone pushed him across the finish line in 28 minutes and 14 seconds. Not bad for a 5-mile run.

All that was left was a 30-minute sparring session, not that it would last that long. Ralph made his way over to the grassy patch where the sparring would take place. Ralph stripped his shirt off, revealing scars across his body. Scars from the fistfights, knife fights, occasional gun fights, and the even less occasional harpoon fights—all from past Black Fridays. His scars covered him from head-to-toe, each reminding him of his victories, as well as rare losses. Those losses, however few, fueled him.

He stepped toward the fighting ground; all the while under the animalistic glare of Pat, his fiercest competitor in the ring but ally on the battlefield, aka the shopping mall.

"Let's go, punk. Move your ass up here!" Honestly one of the nicer greetings Ralph's received from Pat in the sparring ground. It only took a glance at Ralph's scars to realize he had been through a lot, but nonetheless, he dreaded every time he had to box with Pat. Ralph strapped on his gloves and assumed his fighting stance.

They met in the middle and prepared to engage.

Pat lowered her arms and let them hang at her sides. "Come on, you get first punch." Something Pat always did to challenge Ralph.

"DON'T BE A PUSSY!" Pat extended her chin, essentially offering it on a silver platter.

Reluctantly, but fully aware of having no other option, Ralph gritted his teeth and initiated his windup. He reared his fist back as he shifted his weight to his back foot. Then, in one fluid motion, he exploded forward; stepping forward with his left foot while simultaneously rotating his torso and rocketing his stone-solid fist toward the intended target at blistering speed. All these factors culminated to channel Ralph's entire rage and deliver the ultimate blow with cataclysmic force so intense that Ralph closed his eyes because even he couldn't bear to witness the collision.

Pat's chin didn't move an inch. Pat didn't even blink as she snarled with a demonic grin. "Now it's my turn."

Pat unleashed all hell on Ralph. Unloading a hailstorm of right hooks and left uppercuts to Ralph's face, neck, chest, and groin—that's right, Pat fights dirty alright. It took 30 seconds for Pat to have Ralph wheezing, gasping, and cowering in the fetal position, begging for mercy.

"PANZY!" Pat spat on Ralph's back. "You have to be ready for the pain tomorrow, or else, you gonna die, boy. If you ain't ready for Black Friday Eve, you gonna die, boy. Most importantly, if we don't get that Hologram Supreme Dream Watch that's 90%[1] off, and it's

---

[1] The Hologram Supreme Dream Watch was well regarded as the highest-profile item discounted during the year's Black Friday shopping sale. Once activated, the watch would surround the user with a virtual force field, giving the user the phenomena of being transported to a new world, time, location, or situation. Users could utilize the Hologram Supreme Dream Watch to take virtual vacations, interact with their favorite television shows, or take a mental escape from really any situation. The clarity and definition were so incredible that users felt they were actually living these experiences; except all from the comfort of their own home. This watch was a breakthrough for wearable technology. You must remember that this was before surgically-inserted technology was available; and for that matter, before genetically-inserted technology was available. Although the Hologram Supreme Dream Watch is considered an ancient relic by today's standard, it paved the way as an alternative to therapy, anti-depressants, parenting, and other assorted hassles.

your fault, you gonna die, boy." Pat gave Ralph another minute to collect himself. "Get off the ground, you'll be late for school!"

Ralph wanted to lie on the forgiving grass forever, but he knew the consequences if done so. With shaking arms, Ralph hoisted himself up.

"You answer me, boy! I won't take your disrespect."

Still winded, Ralph struggled to open his mouth. "Yes, mother."

Pat relaxed her shoulders and ran her fingers through her long, brunette hair. "Mommy loves you."

Too weak to stand, Ralph began to crawl away.

"I SAID 'Mommy loves you.'"

"Love you, too."

"Say goodbye to your dad and sister before you go."

"Okay." Ralph eventually regained use of his legs, and walked back to the Savers Super Mart, which had been his family's make-shift home for the last few months. The last few months had been brutal living outside of the retail giant. With only a tattered camping tent to call home, there was no personal space, protection from the extreme weather conditions, or amenities to make the last few months even slightly tolerable. With that said, the months of suffering and discomfort and barely getting by would be justified in less than 24 hours. By this time tomorrow, Ralph and his family would be the proud owners of the top product of this year's shopping season. Ralph walked in from the backside of the store so he could pass everyone by in line. In less than 24 hours, all his troubles would disappear. At this time there were about 50,000 people in line, and with each person Ralph passed, he felt an increasing sense of superiority. One by one, he passed by the underachievers that hadn't taken three months off work to wait in line like his family had. He laughed at the lazy, improperly-prioritized losers who thought there were better things to do than wait in line. Idiots. He walked along the line almost all the way to Savers

Super Mart's main entrance, until he saw the teal canvas tent. He peaked his head inside to see his dad, Oscar, acting as a human Barbie doll for Ralph's almost-four-year-old sister, Lauren.

"Oh, hey there, Ralph!" Oscar said with his back still turned.

"Hi Dad, I'm off to school."

"Okay, Ralph. Have a good day."

"Whatever." Ralph tried to walk away before Oscar turned around, but Oscar was too fast.

Oscar turned around, and Ralph saw that Lauren was learning how to apply mascara today. Oscar's face looked like an offshore drilling site that hosted the most recent environmental disaster. Ralph shuddered at the sight. "Whatever. See you after school."

"Woah, woah, now. Not so fast, Mister!" Oscar said as he wagged his finger.

"What?"

"Your hair is an absolute mess. And not in the sexy rebellious actor way, but in the *NO WOMAN WILL EVER MARRY YOU WAY*! Come here. Chop chop."

Ralph begrudgingly knelt down as Oscar licked his fingers and hand-combed Ralph's hair into place. Ralph looked anywhere to avoid looking at his dad. "Well that's a little better."

"I'm going to be late for school."

"Fine, fine. Go. Wait. Are you wearing that to school?" Oscar said, obviously put-off. His eyes beamed holes into Ralph's workout attire: sweaty t-shirt, basketball shorts, and running shoes.

"God! Dad, I seriously need to go to school."

"You're not in that much of a hurry. Seriously son, too many days dressing as a hobo will mean you're never getting married. Ever!"

"Dad, I'm only 12. I don't care about getting married."

"If I didn't know you weren't being serious, I would seriously start crying right now." Oscar fanned his eyes as he started crying, anyways.

"Dad, don't cry. It's pathetic."

"Oh, so it's pathetic for a dad to want his son to be married?" Oscar implored, as he dried his own tears. "I'm just saying, you may not think about being married now, but for guys like us, we aren't afforded that luxury. If you get off to the wrong reputation now, you're done. I'm serious." [2]

"Fine, I'll change." Ralph opened his duffel bag, picked out a polo shirt and swapped it for his t-shirt.

"Good choice with the MuMu Moon[3], Son! Son, I just want you to have all the happiness that I have. Men like us aren't always so lucky."

"Yeah sure, whatever. Bye." Ralph left the tent, trying to erase the image of his mascara'd up father. Not exactly sure if being selected for marriage was all it was hyped up to be.

O   O   O   O   O   O

---

[2] Oscar was correct to be concerned, for every action was recorded through social media. A prime example was the *Hey I'm Pregnant* Pregnancy Test. Upon taking the pregnancy test, the anxious couple would be notified of a positive test result via a Facebook friend request from their just-conceived baby. Given the fact that one's social media accounts covered their entire lifespan, absolutely nothing was hidden from the internet. When choosing a husband, a woman would check his entire history for any embarrassing photos, ill-conceived posts, etc. Any red flags would almost certainly terminate the male's prospects, for women did not want to marry someone that may relapse into past behavior.

[3] MuMu Moon was the premiere sports/casual wear. Consumers paid a premium price for MuMu Moon, which averaged an asking price 10 times higher than comparable brands, just to wear their utter-logoed shirts, shorts, and sweaters, with pride. Even though undercover investigative journalist Dern Vittels previously wrote an exposé piece revealing that MuMu Moon simply pasted their utter logo over their competitor's clothes, the demand for MuMu Moon only grew.

Time for class. Ralph lined up with all the other 12-year-old white boys for class. Ralph attended Parkmere Elementary School, whose full title was Parkmere Elementary School for Lowly Caucasian Males.[4]

Ralph entered the classroom with his classmates, and sat at his respective desk and pulled out his tablet and turned it on. Had to log in by 8:15.

The teacher, Mrs. Kapoor, popped on to their screen at 8:15, with some light Indian music playing and a pristine view of the Himalayas behind her.[5]

"Hello class."

"Hello Mrs. Kapoor."

"I wanted to remind you all that this class is brought to you by Savers Super Mart, *We Sell Absolutely Everything.*"

"Now I'm sure everyone is excited for tomorrow, being Black Friday Eve, but we need to stay focused. For young boys like you, Black Friday season means everything. It may not mean much to you now, but when you are older, you need to be expert shoppers to be selected by a woman. Women must see that you can make the most of their checkbook if they are to be comfortable in choosing you for their husband."

Of course. Everyone knew what was at stake.

"Alright, so let's start with math. Here's the first question."

---

[4] Parkmere was a school exclusively for Kindergarten through 6th-grade males of Caucasian descent. Ralph was born without luck, he was born a white male. His dad told him of a day when white men ruled the world, but that seemed incomprehensible to Ralph. In his 12 years, he had known white men as the bottom of the food chain. After years of passed legislature strengthening diversity hiring measures, it became illegal to hire a white man over either a female or person of minority race in any circumstance.

[5] Several years before this story, American legislators passed a law to outsource all teaching positions to save significant amounts of money. Within a decade, a large majority of these outsourced positions were automated.

The feed of Mrs. Kapoor ended, being replaced with the math problem appearing on the screen.

Top Shop Electronics has a sale, in which:

> *84' Saikamiyahtsu flat screen TVs that cost $2,900 are 60% off*
>
> *Deafstar Mega sound systems that normally cost $1,350 are 50% off*
>
> *Delton Laptops that normally cost $925 are 70% off*
>
> *What is the totally cost, savings, and discount.*

A piece of cake for Ralph and he quickly typed in his answer. *Total Cost: $2,112.50; Savings: $3,062; Discount: 59%.*

Ralph locked in his answer by pressing the "Send to Teacher" button.

Five seconds later, the tablet screen cut back to the teacher. "Good, good job students. I see that was a bit easy for you all. Everyone got that one right. Now, let's study our current events."

The next question appeared on the students' screens.

> *You are shopping for clothes at Savers Super Mart:*
>
> *There's a $90 pair of Rene Gucone tie-dye parachute pants on a 30% discount*
>
> *There's also a $140 pair of Mason Creek silver pinstripe pants for 60% off*
>
> *Which one do you buy? Remember, both your answer and your reasoning need to be correct.*

Leland, the boy next to Ralph hit *Answer* first. Soon after, most of the class had locked in their answer.

Mrs. Kapoor reappeared on the screen, pleased with her class' haste in answering the question. "Leland was the first to answer the question. Leland, do you mind sharing your answer?"

"Well, the Mason Creek pinstripe pants, of course," Leland scoffed at how easy he found this question. "Not only are they the least expensive after discount, but have the highest original price. Therefore, they have the highest perceived value."

Mrs. Kapoor's serene demeanor vaporized as fast as she appeared and disappeared from her students' tablets. "NO! INCORRECT! GO SIT IN THE 'ALONE FOREVER' CORNER! NOW!"

A look of sheer shock and disbelief struck Leland and the rest of the room. "But Mrs. Kapoor, I don't understand. My math is not wrong."

"Your discounting abilities are fine, Leland. What you didn't account for, was that silver has been out of style for months. Pinstripes have been out of style for a decade! Why on earth would your wife want to be walking with her husband, in public, showing the world that she can't even dress him properly? The Rene Gucone tie-dye parachute pants, on the other hand, are well worth it, despite the smaller discount. Remember, a huge discount is pointless if the style will become obsolete. Tie-dye parachute pants will NEVER become obsolete. NEVER!"

"I, I…"

"Leland, thank goodness you are making this mistake now. Because if you are so lucky to be picked as a husband, and if your wife is so generous that she lets you do as much as pick out your own clothes, you better not embarrass her like this. And I mean ever! *Alone Forever* corner, now!"

Leland sulked to the corner, where he had to put on the Costume of Shame, consisting of a fake belly, cracked glasses, and a rainbow-colored hat with a propeller top. And that's how Leland remained for the rest of the four-hour class. It gave Ralph shivers, what if he was left to die, alone. What if no woman picked him?[6]

After the classroom portion of class ended, the students were sent off to the school's gym for their two-hour weight-training session. With all of the disadvantages burdened on them, Caucasian males had to stay conditioned and in top shape if they wanted to catch the eye of a woman.

O   O   O   O   O   O

The family all sat around their tent for their final supper before Black Friday Eve; the night they all dedicated the last few months for preparation. The past few months had been the closest the family had ever been: they ate two meals together every day, there was no technology to get in the way of real human interaction, and there were no separate rooms for the family members to seclude themselves. For once, the Macys felt like an actual family. It was Hell.

The family all waited at the miniature fold-out dinner table. Ralph sat next to his sister and across from his mom/sparring partner. His dad was just taking the entrée out of the oven—microwave oven, that is.

"Just finishing up," Oscar chirped, placing the steaming bowl in front of them all. "And dinner is served." He took the lid off from the pot to reveal dinner, "Hot Pockets served with instant mac 'n' cheese, all fresh out of our portable microwave."

MMMMMMM.

"Wow Dad! Smells good!"

"MMM. Daddy!"

"Aww, thanks kids, glad you like it." The relief on Oscar's face was clear as day. He stressed over the meal every day, a man must

---

[6] At the time of Ralph's worrying, the marriage selection rate for Caucasian males dropped to a dismal 12.9%. Being that Caucasian males had no real job prospects, women were left seeking the attention of ethnic males.

know how to cook a good meal. Oscar looked to the matriarch of the family for the final word on his prepared dinner.

"Yes, my little honeybear, well done on dinner; not that I'm surprised or anything."

"Oh, I am so glad; especially after that fiasco that was last night." Oscar rested his hand on his chest to ease his elevated heartbeat.

"No, no, it wasn't a fiasco, it was just different for my taste, that's all."

"And by different you mean horrible, don't you!" Oscar snapped back.

"Honeybear! Don't be so moody, it was fine." Pat's face softened and she gently rubbed Oscar's shoulder. "Plus, I don't want you stressing about the past; can't have my lil' honeybear getting wrinkles. What's the point of marrying a younger man if no one can tell you're younger?"

"Okay. I'm sorry for acting up," Oscar said. Pat's reassurance alleviated his stress.

"No, answer the question."

This demand clearly caught Oscar off guard, being that he thought Pat previously posed a rhetorical question. "…Well, there is no reason."

"Exactly."

This awkward silence, full of power stares from Pat and suppressed whimpers from Oscar, was finally broken as Oscar failed to realistically act as if he was unscathed by his wife's threat.

"So kids, do you know what tomorrow is?"

"It's Black Friday Eve, duh."

"Yes, but do you know—or DYK, for short—that it used to be something entirely different? It used to be called Thanksgiving."

"Why Daddy? Because we are thankful for Black Friday being one day away?

"Awww, sweetie. Near the end, yes; but it existed before Black Friday even existed."

"Nuh uh. You're lying," Ralph refuted; not even bothering to look up from his phone, which really hurt Oscar. Oscar treasured the times when Ralph used to make eye contact when insulting him.

"I am not, young man. It was about giving appreciation. In fact, stores weren't even open on Thanksgiving."

"WHAT? NO WAY." This statement was shocking enough for Ralph to break his staring contest with his phone, which proved to be quite a nostalgic moment for Oscar. "God, that sounds lame! What's there to be thankful for if stores aren't even open?"

"Nobody knows for sure, but historians believe it was originally a time meant for bonding, and to appreciate family and coming together and good food."

"That's bogus, Dad. You're such a bad liar."

"I am not lying-"

"Honeybear!" Pat interjected, tired of this meaningless debate. "If my son calls you a liar, then you're a liar."

"Ok."[7]

"Anyway, it's not the past that we should be worried about. We need to be focused on tomorrow. Tomorrow is the big day. It's our last Black Friday Eve. A great holiday that will be no more after this year."

"Why does Black Friday have to go away, Mommy?"

---

[7] Historical documents support Oscar's statements. Indeed, there was a time when shopping was not even part of the holiday. However, the validity of these documents have come into question recently. Today's historians believe that most of these claims are based in pure fantasy and are too surreal to be true.

"Because the Chinese are bad, bad people who have no values whatsoever. Or if they have values, they're the wrong ones.[8]

"Well, this was a lot of fun. It was really fun getting to spend all this time together. As long as the Chinese don't mind that we go camping or something."

"Aww sweetie, you don't know what you're talking about. So cute!"

"But really Mommy! We don't need technology to be together."

"Sweetie," Pat said, more sternly. "The joke is old now, cut it out. The Chinese will take all of the fun away."

"But Mommy, why do they take all the fun away?"

"Because they said we were wasting our lives. Saying that we could afford all of these things 10-times-over if we just went to work and saved up.[9] But what those sushi eaters didn't realize, is that they're taking away everything we have to live for. I feel for the little children of your age who grow up not knowing who Bay Raylor was."

"Who's Bay Raylor?"

"Bay Raylor is an American hero, legend, icon, and our greatest president. While in office, he waited a full year in line outside of Savers Super Mart for a 4D printer."

"He waited all of that time for a 4D printer? That's it?"

---

[8] The sale of the former United States of America to China was about to take effect on the first day of the next year. After years of unproductivity due to extended shopping seasons, decreases in educational funding, and increased outsourcing of all American jobs and manufacturing; the former United States fell into an unclimbable pit. With no means to pay off the massive debt, the country declared bankruptcy and was purchased by China, the highest bidder. The Chinese government's first order of business was to cancel Black Friday Eve, Black Friday, and all 44 other major shopping events.

[9] For the final Black Friday season, the average person spent a record-high 23 days waiting outside of their favorite store.

"That's it?" Pat mocked her daughter's response, disgusted that she didn't see the importance of Mr. Raylor's efforts. "That's it?!?"

"Well everyone has a 4D printer now."

"Now, yes. But back then, no one had them. He was the first person in the entire country to get one."

"He waited a year just to be the first person to get one?"

"Yes, that's what I just said."

"Did they only make one 4D printer?"

"No, of course not. They made millions that year, but Bay Raylor was the first to get one that was 70% off. Oh darling Lauren, if only you could see the number of retweets he had. He was on the trending list that day, that glorious day."

"But Mommy, if so many people got one, he didn't have to wait that long, did he?"

"What are you saying? Of course he had to be out there. Millions got one, but he was the first."

"But what about his family, did they wait with him?"

"No, I believe the wife and kids left him, because he 'wasn't providing for the family,'" Pat said in air quotes. "Needless to say, they ended up regretting that choice dearly."

"But isn't family more important than an object?"

"Please child, everybody has a family, or comes from a family. Only one person can ever say they got the first 4D printer, and that man is Bay Raylor." Pat was approaching her boiling point dealing with her family's ignorance. She had to shift the dinner conversation to running over the family's plans for the next day before she completely lost it.

The plan was pretty straightforward: find the Hologram Supreme Dream Watch, secure the Hologram Supreme Dream Watch, and run back because your life depended on it.

The first step was more difficult than it may sound. Savers Super Mart was a massive store; running several football fields in either direction.[10] Savers Super Mart announced that they would have 30 Hologram Supreme Dream Watches available at this location. Although the company did not disclose the exact location, Pat was able to extract this intel from a lonely cashier. According to Pat's source, the 30 watches would be split up evenly; 15 on the far-right back corner of the store and 15 on the far-left back corner of the store.

The watches being so far away from the entrance certainly favored the athletically-superior Macys. They would overtake several of the slower shoppers and when they reached the watch display, there wouldn't be nearly as much pandemonium as when the top display stands are right at the opening of the store. There were 87 people in-front of them, but not all of them were shopping for the Hologram Supreme Dream watch, and several were not nearly in good-enough shape to beat Pat in a foot race; so the Macys were confident in being able to secure four watches. To improve their odds, the Macys agreed to split up; Pat and Lauren would travel left and the Macy boys would head to the right.

Now, the third step was the trickiest. On the journey back to the cash registers, located at the front of the store, the Macys would have to race through a stampede of shoppers—entering the store at a rate of over 300 people per minute—without getting killed or stripped of their possessions. In addition, of the 30 watches on sale, only the first 10 would be available at a discount—a 90% discount! Listed at a $200,000 retail price, the first 10 watches would be available for only $20,000 each. For this reason, it was a blessing in disguise that the Macys chose to camp out for so long because they were kicked out of

---

[10] The modern Savers Super Marts were the size of small towns; and if all the stores in the former United States were combined, Savers Super Mart would be the 12th largest state in the country. The megastore used its sheer size and volume to engulf the competition and run any rivals out of business. Initially thought of as a retail discounter, Savers Super Mart expanded to selling absolutely every product and service available. This included everything from toilet paper and duct tape, to yachts and luxury cars. Some of the larger stores even had a 9-hole golf course.

their house for failing to make payments since the previous Black Friday season cleaned them out.

The whole family felt content with their plans in place. The mutual silence served as Oscar's cue to start clearing the table of paper napkins and plates. As he passed around the table, Pat squeezed him on the backside.

Pat reacted as if she had taken a bite out of a lemon. "Honeybear, did you work out today?"

"No, I was busy doing paperwork around the house. Is something wrong?" Oscar responded with alarm.

"No Honeybear…just felt a little soft back there."

"I'm so sorry baby, I'll start working out this instant!" Oscar set down the disposable tableware in his arms and dropped to the floor to start doing some clapping push-ups as if his life depended on it.

"There's my honeybear," Pat smirked at how easy it was to manipulate her partner.

Ralph oversaw this entire exchange and didn't like how his mom treated his dad, but that's just the way the world was—a heterosexual white man had no prospects or value in the world except for the entertainment he could provide his wife.

The giant clock tower from the once-church-now-watch emporium rang eight times.

"Okay people," Pat said. "Time for bed."

Ralph, Lauren, and Oscar laid down in their respective sleeping bags as Pat looked over them. "It's going to be a dogfight out there tomorrow, so make sure to have sweet dreams prying those watches out of the other shoppers' hands. By any means, murder if necessary."

"But Mommy, I don't want to kill anyone."

"Oh Sweetie, so naïve. You may not want to kill now, but just wait until you see that Hologram Supreme Dream Watch for the first time. You'll be ready to kill for it then."

"But Mommy, I don't want to die for a watch."

"Sweetie, what did I say about you saying stupid things? You just don't realize how great it will be. When we all have our own watches, we won't have to spend a single second together again. We'll be able to take our own virtual vacations, and with their 360-degree screen and noise-cancelling technology, we can be sitting right next to each other and not know each other even exists! Now that is something worth fighting for."

"But-"

"That's enough now, Lauren. Go to bed, NOW!"

Lauren joined her dad and brother on the ground and willed herself to sleep.

Soon, it was just Pat that was awake; looking straight ahead to Savers Super Mart's main entrance a couple hundred feet away. She also saw the 87 people in line in front of them. She kicked herself knowing that they should have camped out earlier. She soothed herself, reminding herself that all the members weren't all going for the same items. The Hologram Supreme Dream Watch may be the marquee item this year, but a store like Savers Super Mart had plenty of big-ticket items. The Pedrozas were waiting for the jumbo gym set. The Systerons, among the first 20 people in line, were camped out for one of three luxury cars on sale for 80% off. As their daughter's only wish for her Sweet 16 next year, the parents needed to be able to secure a discounted luxury car—now more than ever since both parents had been laid off due to their several-month absence from work. Of the 87 people in front of the Macys, Pat calculated that only 58 were going for the hologram watch. Of those 58, the mentally-weak would get distracted or discouraged. Others lack the physical speed, power, and ferocity to beat out Pat and her family. However, there still remained 36 shoppers in front of the Macys that would be in the lead for the 10 watches on sale. Pat didn't back down from the challenge, but she

knew of her restrictions. She was 38, and although the owner of
bulging biceps, gazelle-fast limbs, and washboard abs that could, and
have, served as an actual washboard; she was aging. The competition
would be especially intense; even bigger this year than the last. Pat
looked behind her to see a line that the news stations had reported to
be around 75,000. One last hurrah for the American consumer. Savers
Super Mart was by no means the only store with an impressive
offering; every store offered discounts of 90%+ off their major items.
For the final year though, anyone who was anyone shopped at Savers
Super Mart. In attempt to gain a first-mover advantage, some stores
even opened as early as 8pm on Wednesday to catch shoppers'
attention. Even with a four-hour head start, none of the stores could
capitalize because no one would sacrifice their spot in line for Savers
Super Mart.

The clock struck 11:59pm, and the murmuring amidst the
crowd reached a fever pitch.

Pat pulled her just-woken family into a circle. "Everyone, stay
calm. We've been training all year for this. We're going to have to split
up, but as soon as we lock down Eagle One, we move."

The giant clock tower initiated its first of twelve rings, but no
one could hear the other eleven. The automated entrance way[11] lifted,
making Savers Super Mart up for the taking. The first few crawled
under the rising gates. The whole line pushed forward in unison. The
stream of shoppers crawling in led to a running of the bulls as the gates
rose all the way. The Macys shoved their way in and ran in their
assigned directions.

With less than a hundred people entering the store before her,
Pat ran through the aisles uninhibited, passing plenty of great deals
along the way: socks for a nickel, child swing set for $9, designer
watches for $32; all deals for the weak. All she needed to remember
was the time 8 years ago, when she settled for the practical diamond

---

[11] The entry ways for all Savers Super Marts became completely automated after the
previous year's infamous *Black Friday Eve* trampling, which is still known as the
deadliest event in American history.

earrings, instead of fighting for the bedazzled pimp cane, which was the featured sale item that year. She figured, it was there, it was more practical, and it served a purpose. But she suffered the agony of seeing her nemesis, Gabriela Esperanza, flaunt around her pimp cane. When Pat got 49 Facebook likes, 39 Instagram likes, and 21 retweets; Gabriela got 114, 99, and 103; respectively. It was an utter embarrassment. Also, it was the last time Pat let practicality and responsibility get in her way of a killer deal.

Pat continued forward with her daughter strapped to her back. It was no doubt impeding her speed though. There was no way she'd make up ground with a 38 lb. sand bag attached to her. Pat looked around for an alternate route. Any other way would take them off of the fastest path to the hologram watches, but they still had about 300 yards to go. Pat diverged from the pack of shoppers making a beeline to the Hologram watches, making a sharp left turn into the sports section. She zoned in on the bike section and took out the first two-seat bicycle she could find. She peeled Lauren out from her strap and plopped her down on the back bicycle seat.

"Put on this helmet. Put your feet on the pedals and hold on tight!"

"Mommy, I'm scared!"

"It's OK Lauren, we'll get those watches! I'll be right back."

Pat ran over to the next aisle to the beach section to grab a beach umbrella and returned to her daughter and vehicle.

"Alright, let's go!" Pat hopped onto the lead seat and started her pedaling motion while still air bound—eager to make up for lost time. The detour had placed the female contingent farther behind, but it gave hope that they would catch up even quicker.

Ahead, she saw the illuminated and elevated golden display holding the west side's 15 Hologram Supreme Dream Watches. Yet on the rotating case, she only saw two left; the west side was heavily targeted by shoppers. Even if she managed to snag the last two, the chances of her and Lauren being among the first 10 to purchasers to

reach the checkout stand would be slim to none. A split-second was all
the time Pat had to decide on Lauren and her next move. Lauren and
Pat had three options: race for the final 2 watches on display and run
like hell back to the cash registers, concede the big sale and make a
killing on the hundreds of other great deals in the store, or find some
people with two watches and abduct the sale items from their original
owners. Really there was only one option.

O   O   O   O   O   O

Ralph and Oscar made their way across the east side of the
store. Ralph had his Savers Super Mart app[12] onscreen to help him
locate the mythical hologram watches. The app led him to where he
needed to go. His dad and he dashed to the golden display, still with 11
left. It seemed eerily quiet. Too quiet.

A woman, watch in hand, began her trek back to the cash
registers. Ralph made eye contact with her, but with plenty of watches
left on display, there was no benefit for either side to engage in a fist
fight.

The unchallenged traverse to the watch display troubled Ralph
and Oscar. It was way too quiet.

A whooshing sound snuck up on Ralph. He instinctively
ducked. Something shattered against the alcohol aisle behind them—
flooding the floor with cheap red wine.

"Ralph! Duck!" Oscar yelled.

They both ducked as a dozen more metallic circular discs sliced
up the air surrounding them. One struck the woman in the neck,

---

[12] The Savers Super Mart Map app originated as a way to catch the recent trends of all
the stores having an app to notify shoppers of upcoming deals, price alerts, item
availability, and more. As the average Savers Super Mart continued to grow
exponentially in size, the map feature became a near-necessity. With the average store
growing beyond 2.5 million square feet, obese shoppers, Savers Super Mart's top
demographic, became incensed with the amount of exercise the had to do to get what
they needed. Also, Savers Super Mart was forced to react to a string of deaths during
one summer in which people died of exhaustion, not knowing how to get out of the
store.

sending her hurdling into the ground. Another disc—still intact—skid against the ground until sliding into Ralph. He looked over at the 6-inch metallic disk, which had a pink top, and bared an image of a scantily-clad girl and was labelled *Oops, I did it again.*

"Dad, what are these?"

"They're some kind of Chinese throwing star! Watch out!"[13]

"Who's the woman in pink?"

"She must be their supreme queen, or something."

"We have to move."

The father-son duo rushed to the golden display. More of the strange discs whirled their way. They were moving fast enough to miss the bulk of the onslaught, but the discs that connected with skin, stung. Finally they reached the stand and grabbed the two watches. As the pair turned to sprint back, they were met by two punks, with steak knives inches away from Oscar's and Ralph's necks.

"Hand'em over," said one of the goons.

Oscar was startled, knowing everyone had to pass through metal detectors. Then he realized the kitchen section was just a couple aisles away.

"Woah, we—." Oscar said in a faux-startled tone.

As if in a vicious synchronized dance competition, Oscar and Ralph kicked their respective attackers in their respective groins and gut-punched them as they crumpled in mind-numbing pain. To finish

---

[13] The weapons being hurled at them were called compact discs, which used to be known simply as CDs. CDs served a similar purpose as the music players of today; except you needed a music player, or CD player, to play them. Unlike today where the music player is attached to your eardrum, past users used earphones to listen to music.

them off, the Macy boys spun clockwise and roundhouse-kicked the attackers' weapons away.

By the time the Macy boys disposed of their attackers, a few dozen shoppers stood frozen around them. Oscar and Ralph cleared the way with a power stare; no one wanted to mess with them after that impressive display.

O   O   O   O   O   O

With her mind made up, Pat zeroed in on the target: a man running back proudly with two Supreme Dream Watches. She charged full-steam at the man. The man looked up just in time to see the pink two-seater coming his way, but not soon enough to do anything about it. Pat steered slightly to the left of the man and swung the umbrella under him, sweeping his feet out from underneath him. The knock left the man sprawling forward onto his belly and sent the two watches flying into the air and sliding away. Pat slammed on the breaks, sending the two-seater into a full-out drift until it reached a screeching halt. Pat dismounted the bicycle and lunged Superman-style over to the two watches, grasping both.

Her maternal instincts rang within her, to make sure her baby wasn't hurt. She had a strong instinct that her baby was injured. So with haste, she picked up the box and examined the corners, it was perfect, if not minutely crumpled along the corners. Pat drew a sigh of relief, her baby had survived.

"Alright Lauren, we gotta go. Wait, one second." Pat snatched her phone out of her purse and threw it to Lauren.

"LAUREN, I need you to listen very carefully. Take a picture of me with my watches and upload it to Instagram NOW! The message should read: *Check out who got a golden watch, bitches, #blackfriday #Ivegotthegoldenticket #-*

"Not so fast!"

Pat saw that the man she just tripped up had recovered and held Lauren in his arms. Pat noticed he was wearing a *World's Best Dad* t-shirt.

"Oh my God!"

"Just give me the watch."

"Just push *Send*, Lauren, push *Send*, for God's sake."

This was not the reaction that World's Best Dad was expecting.

"Lauren, push send now! I don't care if you didn't get the last hashtag!"

"Wait, seriously? I have your daughter."

"Oh my God, give it back."

"I will, just give me that little toy you're holding and I'll give your daughter back safe and sound."

"I'm talking about my phone, you retard!"

"Lady, do you not see that I have your daughter—"

"I pressed send Mommy!"

"Oh my God, baby, I've never been so proud of you before. I love you!"

"Lady, I'm holding your freaking daughter, doesn't that concern you?"

"Will you not shut up? Just give my daughter back, you kidnapper!"

"I will. I won't kidnap your daughter, I just want the watches. Please!"

"Are you serious? You need to get a life, pal." Pat didn't notice any contradiction in her statement.

"If I don't bring home at least one watch, I have nothing to live for. If I get this, my wife said she'd let me back in the house."

Pat couldn't stand to see this man holding her crying daughter (because Lauren was an ugly crier and made the most hideous sounds), but she also saw the crowd focus in on her. She had to dash.

"I want my daughter back!"

"Then just give me the watch, and I'll give her back."

"I love my daughter!"

"Then trade her back, NOW!"

"But my love for my one and only daughter cannot compare to how much I love this watch." As her last word left her mouth, Pat started backing away. Leaving World's Best Dad more than befuddled.

"You'd leave your daughter in the hands of a stranger with possible violent intentions, for a watch?"

"My daughter, Lauren, is exactly 4 years old, today. She was born on Black Friday four years ago. She couldn't be born one day earlier or even one day later. She had to be born on Black Friday. I tried to go anyway to the sales, but the doctor held me back. Told me I couldn't go. That year, I missed out on everything. Since that day, I promised myself that I would never let someone get in the way of me and a sale. I love my daughter, but I would rather keep my word." Pat ran off, not planning on seeing that man, or her daughter, again. She chuckled to herself, overjoyed to have essentially traded the weight off her shoulders for two of the prized watches.

O   O   O   O   O   O

As Oscar and Ralph rushed back, they saw a never-ending horde heading their way. Word must be out that the watch display on the other side is empty.

"Those two have watches! Get them!"

"If they see us with these watches, we'll never make it back."

"We can just say we don't have them."

"But then, we won't make the discount cut. We have no time for hesitation!"

They each scanned the room, and both thought the same thing at the same time and voiced their decision in unison. "Up!"

Oscar and Ralph climbed up the nearest aisle and rolled on top just as the horde reached them. As they stealthily crept along the aisle-top, one shopper spotted them.

"They're on top of the aisle, get them!"

Oscar and Ralph started an all-out sprint to get back to the cash registers. Everything people could find was thrown at them. This wasn't so bad when they ran through the bedroom section because throw pillows were easy to dodge; but in the outdoor section, rakes and shovels proved not nearly as forgiving.

The training began to really show its purpose. All the objects thrown at them might have slowed down lesser men, but not them. All those sessions Pat beat Ralph to a pulp gave him the perseverance to run through the hailstorm of discounted goods.

"We're almost there, Dad!" Through the barrage of pens and books and lamps, Ralph saw the cash registers only a mere 50 yards away.

"Go! Son! Go! Head down and GO! Watch out from the left!"

"Ralph looked back at his dad to see where he was looking, then he realized a frightening truth: they were passing by the gun section.

"Oh no!"

A dozen or so shoppers, most likely around the $7,000^{th}$ or so to enter the store, were obviously going with the sniper strategy—just sit back in the firearms section and pluck off anyone you wanted the merchandise of.

Shots were fired, with only one striking Oscar in the shoulder.

"Keep going!"

More shots were fired. Then a lull struck in the firing.

Ralph looked to his left and gasped with horror.

A little girl, no older than 9, was holding her sparkly pink rocket launcher.

Oscar shook his head, of course this would have to be the first year of the child-friendly bazookas.[14]

"COVER YOUR EARS!"

The little girl fired, causing the traffic of thousands to wince at the searing noise. The missile rocketed toward Oscar and Ralph. Ralph froze as he watched the missile rocket straight at him. Just as impact was about to occur, Oscar tackled Ralph from behind, sending them to the right, descending on the furious crowd that has tried so furiously to bring them down. Nanoseconds later, the missile collided with the aisle, on its top shelf. Three feet higher and it would've taken out one of them. All around them, shrapnel sprayed throughout the crowd, leaving the mob in disarray for fleeting moments. Although both were wounded, the Macys capitalized on the chaos and escaped from the angry mob.

O   O   O   O   O   O

Pat continued to sprint and finally saw the cash machines in sight. She examined the crowd to see anyone with gold watches; she knew she'd be cutting it close. She saw two people sporting a Hologram watch and celebrating as they passed through the electronic

---

[14] The child-sized bazooka and multiple similar products came about due to the Child's Right to Bear Arms Act that passed earlier in the year. The Child's Right to Bear Arms Act gave preschoolers the right to use a firearm. In the years to follow, the freedom to bear firearms was expanded through the Universal Right to Bear Arms Act, which allowed absolutely all people in America to bear arms, including convicts (both currently and formerly incarcerated), terrorists, mentally insane, and all varieties of unsavory humans.

cash registers. That meant there were no more than 8 watches remaining for the sale price.

Continuing to scan the crowd, Pat saw the minutest of glints in a man's pocket. He had one watch concealed. If there were even on-sale hologram watches left, this shopper may have the 10th watch, therefore being the final person able to take advantage of this discount of a lifetime. The man was two people from the front of the line. That means Pat had less than 10 seconds to do something before the man completed his e-transaction. Pat cocked back the umbrella and aimed. Aim too short and she'd impale the golden hologram shopper, which would free up the watch, but just for a second before the next shopper snatches it and buys it herself. But throw too far and she'd miss the register all together. With no time remaining, Pat launched the closed umbrella and watched it sail all the way to the register; destroying the register on contact. With all other lines 20-people deep already, the man was screwed.

Pat ran to the cash machine directly next to it, finding a man waiting impatiently in line. Pat slid right up to him.

"Hey hunny, I made it!"

"The man turned, opening his mouth in shock. As soon as he was about to speak, Pat wrapped around him in an embrace while delivering a concealed punch below the belt.

The man hunched over, winded.

"Oh baby, are you okay?"

The man gasped for breath as he fell to the floor, but remained in the fetal position.

Pat turned to the register, just needing to scan the watch.

"PAT!"

Pat saw her husband and son rushing toward her.

"You made it!"

"Yes we did!"

The onlookers stared in puzzlement, thinking the previous man was Pat's husband.

"It's okay, we're Mormon."

This being a seemingly suitable explanation, the Macys were left at peace to scan their items.

This was the moment of truth, either the four watches would come in at a manageable $20,000 each, or would balloon to full price— a completely out-of-reach $200,000 per watch.

Pat scanned all four watch boxes by the scanner. The scanner screen flashed:

Processing

Processing

Processing

4 Hologram Supreme Dream Watches X $200,000.00=$800,000.00

After Discount: $80,000

Savings: $720,000

The Macys rejoiced momentarily. They would be able to take home their prize. It took them to their last of 10 credit cards, and brought their savings account to the single digits, but they had just enough to buy the coveted watches.

Before the Macys left the pay terminals, Pat pulled them into a small hallway leading into the Savers Super Mart employee break room.

"We did it!" Ralph exclaimed.

Ralph's parents shushed him, not wanting to risk any additional attention.

Oscar took a half-minute to make a family headcount. "Hunny, where's Lauren?"

"There's no time for that, Oscar," Pat hissed. Then she calmed herself and snuggled against her husband's arm. "Hey Honeybear, put on the watch, you'll look so sexy!" Pat said in a soft voice as she cuddled up to Oscar.

"But Pat, people will see me, it will put us all in danger."

"Oh don't be paranoid, you can cover it with your sleeve, you sexy man, you."

"Ah, you haven't talked to me like that in forever." Finally Oscar was receiving the attention he had been ever so craving.

"Yeah, yeah, just put it on already."

Oscar obliged and slid the golden watch around his wrist and let go of his sleeve so it would cover up the prize.

Pat, Ralph, and Oscar walked outside, bundling up to hide themselves and any purchases. There were still over 60,000 people yet to enter the store. None of the Macys had ever been this nervous or straight-out horrified before. Menacing spectators watched each shopper to leave the store. Without a doubt, the first people to leave must have something special.

"Just look straight forward," Oscar urged.

"HEY!"

In the corner of his eye, Ralph could see a lady holding up her phone with *Binoculars*[15] running.

"HEY! It's the woman from the Instagram post, she has a hologram watch."

A crowd circled around the Macys and started closing in.

---

[15] *Binoculars* was an extremely popular smartphone app. *Binoculars* was thought of as a huge innovation in face-recognition technology that allowed users to recognize a person's name and bio by matching up a picture of them with their social media profiles. The user of the app would just have to take a picture of anyone and *Binoculars* would pull up all of the available data on the particular individual.

Pat appeared frantic, but to Ralph she had a tinge of collectivity in the glint of her eye; she was up to something.

"We got the tenth one, he has it!" Pat reached over to Oscar and pulled up his left sleeve, exposing the golden glowing hologram watch. "Get him!"

Pat kicked her husband toward the mob. Previously wounded from gun shots, Oscar posed no match toward the swarming hive of aggressors.

Unphased, Pat turned to her son. "Hurry, this bought us time, but we need to move, now!"

Pat and Ralph walked briskly, but calmly, to avoid detection. They parked at the far edge of the Savers Super Mart parking lot; which required a 25-minute walk, or a four-minute sprint, by Pat's standards. Pat and Ralph snuck across the lot, careful to avoid any street lights. By now, rumor must have spread that they both had watches, and there's plenty of sore losers to be worried about. It took a while to get to their parking spot, especially with all of the covert weaving through the lines of parked vehicles. When they arrived at their car, however, it would be a quick exit—avoiding any potential gridlock and risk.

As they continued along their covert walk, more and more cars could be heard prowling up and down the parking aisles. Perhaps the cars just belonged to early birds who were leaving with their haul. Perhaps they were just-arriving shoppers looking for the closest spot available so they could pick through the few items remaining at Savers Super Mart. Still, Pat couldn't help but wonder, what if they were hunting Pat and Ralph?

"Howdy there, leavin' Savers Super Mart already?" asked a woman's voice with a sweet southern accent.

Pat and Ralph practically jumped out of their socks. "Jesus!"

Behind them was a Prius driver. The Prius, silent at under 5 MPH, was undetectable, even for Pat's expertly-trained ears.

"Sorry, didn't mean to scare y'all." The driver, a woman with a kind smile, looked sincere. "Y'all must have gotten a big ticket item to be leaving this early.

Not missing a beat, Pat recovered from her unusual scare. "Oh, we wish. Just walking to the car to get some snacks. We are still a ways back in line."

"Well, we're just getting here, as you can see," the woman said, motioning to her golden retriever riding shotgun. "Want a lift to your car?"

"Oh no, we couldn't. You two need to get in line."

"Oh please, we aren't in a rush; if you couldn't already tell," the woman giggled a very pleasant care-free laugh; which built a nice catalyst to Pat trusting her. "By the way, my name is Sue."

Pat's trust for the lady grew further; Sue was such an innocent and pleasant name.

Pat was deeply considering taking the ride. Not because she was tired or fatigued. Pat ran 10 miles for breakfast (literally; she hadn't eaten breakfast in months). But she grew anxious with the rising number of cars on the prowl. It would be at least 15 more minutes. Surely by now, all the watches have been taken up. Here they were posed with an excellent opportunity to escape under the cover of a friendly woman named Sue.

"Well if it's no trouble—"

"It's no trouble, you silly goose. Get in; come on." Sue waved them in.

Despite Ralph's troubled looks, Pat nodded with approval that it was okay.

Pat and Ralph jumped into the back seat.

Ralph desperately wanted to ask his mom why she fed Oscar—and most likely Lauren—to the wolves. However after seeing Pat's actions, he feared that she would leave him stranded with the slightest bit of defiance.

"Well thank you very much, Sue. I'm Anna Barnard and this is my son…Alph."

"Well isn't that special. It sure is nice to meet you." Sue's smile remained glued to her face. Pat noticed Sue looking down at her phone and was using the *Driving* app[16]. She accelerated a bit, above 10 miles per hour; triggering the safety locks.

"We're just down near the edge of the parking lot, to the left."

"Okie dokes." Sue continued to accelerate.

"Yes, the turn is coming up right after the next row."

"Okie dokie!" Sue chimed, as she continued to accelerate toward the lot exit.

"No, left! I said make a left!" Pat demanded, sounding more distressed than angry.

"Oh my apologies," Sue said, slowing down. "Before I take y'all back to your car, let me just make y'all a bit more comfy." Sue pressed a red button on the central console labeled *Lock*. All of a sudden, a bulletproof glass screen came up; dividing the driver's row from the back row.

"What is this?"

"Ah darling, I don't believe I'll be taking you to your car anytime soon."

"What are you doing?"

---

[16] Back when driving cars was not an automated process, *Driving* was a very popular app for the smartphone and tablet. A simple app, *Driving* had a hooked up view as if the driver was looking through their windshield. *Driving* was thought of as a breakthrough for the time as it allowed users to keep an eye glued to their device while still focusing on the road.

"Oh how dumb do you think I am? You think I don't have *Binoculars*?" Pat flashed her phone's screen; showing Pat's Instagram picture.

"Mom, are you serious? You posted an Instagram while shopping?"

"Oh don't give me that Ralph. It all ended up perfectly timed. Plus look, 39 likes already! That was less than 1 hour ago!"

"Mom! Focus! We're trapped!"

"Your son sure is a bright one. And if you are thinking of breaking your way out, don't even. You are completely surrounded by bulletproof glass. Ain't no escapin' this mess."

"Where are you taking us?"

"Oh, wouldn't you like to know."

Sue caught Pat inching out her phone.

"Oh, and don't even try to call for help, I have a reception blocker in the back compartment."

"You're an evil genius, I can't believe you're kidnapping us!"

"Why thank you."

"Why are you doing this? You're not evil, you're a sweetheart, right? I mean your name is Sue, for Christ's sake, I've never met a Susan that isn't anything but a genuine sweetheart."

"Oh, I forgot to mention that I go by Sue, but my full first name is Ursula," she cackled quite evilly.

"That is an evil name!" Pat squealed; deceived.

A few miles later, Sue eased the brakes, bringing the car to a halt in what seemed to be an abandoned industrial park.

"What are you going to do to us?" Despite the training, Ralph couldn't hold back his fear of uncertainty.

Right then, a truck rammed into the backside of the car; shoving the car into the intersection, and smashing into an oncoming car.

The collision was so intense that it cracked open the passenger doors containing Pat and Ralph. Regaining consciousness, Pat kicked down the door, and Ralph followed behind her as Pat exited the wrecked vehicle.

Except for the two cars, the roads were clear; everyone was still out shopping. Pat led her son into a nearby decrepit factory building. Footsteps trailed Pat and Ralph but neither wasted any time finding out who was behind them.

Heads ringing, Pat and Ralph stumbled through the semi-open door.

"Hey!"

Pat didn't even bother to turn, but she distinctly noticed two sets of footsteps; two people were on their tails. "Don't look back, just go!" She prodded her son on.

They crawled inside the door and Pat kicked it closed behind them.

As soon as the door slammed closed, Pat checked her purse; both watches were still okay.

"Oh thank goodness."

Suddenly, the door busted open. Pat rounded her back in attempt to shield her prized possession from the intruder; squatting over the watch as if it were one ring to rule it all. Still in the squatting position, Pat pivoted to see the intruder. She dropped the watch, and her bottom jaw, when she saw who stood in the doorway.

It was World's Best Dad standing alongside Lauren.

"You stop following us this instance, sir," Pat begged.

"The offer still stands. I have not hurt a single hair on your daughter's head. Just give me a Hologram watch, and I'll give her back, no harm done," World's Best Dad pleaded.

"NEVER! I will not negotiate!"

"Don't you want your daughter back?"

"I do, but not at this price."

"Seriously woman, I'll pay you triple what you bought 'em for, I just want to bring two watches home."

"No deal."

World's Best Dad stood for tense moments. His grip tightened around Lauren's right arm. "That Hologram Supreme Dream Watch is the only thing that can keep my family together. It's the only thing that will keep my wife from divorcing me. I want to keep my family together, but—," World's Best Dad unclenched Lauren, releasing her to rejoin her family. "But I won't let it ruin another family."

A tearful Lauren ran into Pat's arms, but Pat's arms were firmly grasping the three Hologram Supreme Dream Watches. After Lauren's persistence in hugging her mom, Pat carefully set each one down before opening her arms for her daughter.

World's Greatest Dad skulked out of the room and closed the door behind him. Ralph ran over to give his sister a hug.

"Wow, Mom! You're brilliant. I thought Lauren would never return, but you knew all along!"

Pat would not break her deep gaze with the Hologram watches. "Huh?"

"I said that's amazing how you knew that the man wouldn't go through with kidnapping Lauren. You're a genius!"

"Oh," Pat took a few seconds for the comment to register. "Oh yeah, yeah, I knew the man would return Laura."

"You mean Lauren?"

"What did I say?"

"Laura."

"Oh yeah? Ha-ha, slip of the tongue," Pat said; not wanting to break her gaze with the watches.

After embracing her brother, Lauren looked around and asked, "Where's Daddy?"

"Oh who knows where your dad is; that silly man."

"Mom, you sacrificed him outside the store so we could get away; remember?"

Pat finally looked up from the watches, royally irritated that her kids once again distracted her. "Oh please, stop making such a big deal out of that. I'm sure he's fine."

"But Mom, those people had bats in their hands. What if Dad got beaten to death?"

"Daddy's dead?"

"God! You two and your constant bitching. If I said he was dead, would that put your mind at ease and get you both to shut up?"

"Daddy's dead?"

"Oh just shut it. Anyway, we all have our own Hologram Supreme Dream Watches now; so we don't even need him anymore. Think about it, it's a better father anyway. The watch doesn't complain, it cuts down on vacation money, it doesn't take up excessive space."

Pat couldn't find a discernable change in her children's demeanor, so she busted open one of the watch cases. The watch glimmered as Pat lifted it from its case. With the tiniest bit of natural light, the watch illuminated the immediate air around them; and more importantly, distracted the Macy kids. Leave it to Pat to benefit from the kids' generation's short attention span. Pat seized the opportunity.

"Let's not talk about the past, kids. Now," Pat appealed; gathering the three watches in her arms. "Now we have all that we'll ever need."

The family joined in a 3-way embrace around their new possessions.

"I found you guys," Oscar said; hunched over from exhaustion. In all of the excitement, no one had noticed Oscar limping his way into the abandoned factory. Oscar continued to limp toward the family. "You're all that I'll ever need, too."

Pat, Ralph, and Lauren remained deep in their embrace; not paying any attention to the stranger in the background.

Cutting Room Floor

Eggplant tore the giftwrap off the long, slender box and punched through the thin cardboard. His eyes ballooned as his eyes confirmed what he hoped was inside.

"WOW! A NEW BASEBALL BAT!"

Eggplant's whole body exuded pure joy as he pulled the junior-sized aluminum bat out of its case. His dad continued to capture this precious moment of his 7-year-old on his camcorder.

"What do you think of your birthday present, Eggplant?" his dad said, keeping the camcorder glued on the celebrant.

"THIS IS THE BEST DAY OF MY LIFE!"

Adam and Sarah, known by Eggplant as Dad and Mom, both chuckled.

"I'm so glad you like it." Mom smiled with the same radiance of the pearl necklace and pearl earrings decorating her neck and face. Mom walked into the living room with the birthday boy's cake— careful not to get any frosting on her pretty red spring house dress that looked straight from the 50s. She smiled as if the perfect gift for her son was an even bigger gift for her.

"CAN I PLAY WITH IT?"

"Of course, right after we have cake."

"Aww, but I want to play with it now," Eggplant whimpered with pained eyes and slouched shoulders. "Please?"

Dad pivoted with the handheld camera to look back at Mom. "I don't know dear, I think we can hold off for fifteen seconds, give him his first swing with the new bat."

Mom was hesitant, but her smile shown through. "Okay, one pitch though, then you have to blow out your candles."

"OH BOY!" Eggplant shot out of his Indian-style sitting position and bounced to his feet.

"Come on Dad, throw me a pitch!"

"Ok Son, just let me set the camcorder down, so we can catch this on tape." Dad stepped to his left and placed the camcorder on the table, setting it far enough away so you could see him, Eggplant, and Sarah all in one shot.

"Adam, you better stand in front of me. The ball better not smash up this cake that I spent all morning on."

"Okay dear," Adam said, stepping directly between Sarah and Eggplant. "Ready Son?"

"Ready Dad!" Eggplant assumed his right-handed stance; gently swinging his bat back and forth over his right shoulder, mimicking his idol, Mike Trout.

"Alright." Adam initiated his wind-up, finishing off with a soft underhand pitch, right into Eggplant's strike zone.

Eggplant squared up and unloaded on the pitch, hitting the ball on the sweet spot. The ping was loud and the ball ricocheted off his bat making a beeline directly into Adam's crotch. Adam hunched over, grabbing his crotch, while the sheer force of the ball shoved him back off his feet as he fell backwards. Sarah attempted to move out of the way, but could not clear the area before Adam's head came down on the edge of the birthday cake, catapulting the blue-and-red frosted cake into the air, spinning as it came back down to Earth and landed on the right side of Adam's face.

Eggplant cupped his mouth in disbelief, "Are you okay, Dad?"

Adam groaned, but managed a "Yeah, I'm okay."

"Was that a home run, Dad?"

"No," Adam grimaced with his hands still glued to his crotch, "I think that was ball two."

"Annndd cut!" Adam exclaimed, sitting up and wiping the cake off his face, revealing a now carefree demeanor.

"That was marvelous, dear," Sarah said, fairly pleased, "this was our best take yet."

"Yeah Mom and Dad, that was awesome," Eggplant chimed in.

"It was better, it was not good enough," said Adam, unamused.

"But dear, everything in that take went perfectly: everyone knew their lines, Eggplant hit you right in the crotch, and the cake hit you right in the face. I think we found a keeper."

"No, no, no," Adam barked. "This is not the take. Don't get me wrong, it was better than the others, but there were still way too many mistakes: everyone's timing was off; Eggplant, your lines felt forced; and the cake needs to land directly on my face. If we send in this cut to *AMHHV*, I guarantee we won't get the $250,000 grand prize. Even the $5,000 weekly prize might be out of reach."

Adam was referring to *America's Most Hilarious Home Videos*, which was the top show on television and live-streaming devices. As its title suggests, each weekly episode features funny home videos submitted by American families. At the end of each episode, viewers and audience members voted for their favorite video aired during the show. The family with the best video won a $5,000 check and a finalist spot on the season's final show where the first-, second-, and third-place finishers raked in a sum of $250,000, $75,000, and $25,000, respectively.

Adam plugged in the camcorder to the living room TV to review the most recent take. Adam, Sarah, and Eggplant sat down in their director's chairs titled *Director*, *Star Talent*, and *Junior Talent*; respectively.

"Alright, let's see how it turned out."

As soon as Adam clicked *Play*, Eggplant knew this wouldn't be the take. Adam's mild displeasure grew to disgust, which evolved to pure hatred. Adam reacted so violently to certain miscues that it looked like he was physically abused by the bad acting. Even Sarah's blissful face sunk into a frown during the 45-second clip. Eggplant could tell from their facial expressions that they both grew less and less pleased with the take, Take 6. Eggplant didn't like to see his parents disappointed, but he didn't necessarily mind doing another take. This is the most time he'd spent with his parents in a long time. He didn't mind another take at all. He was actually looking forward to it.

Adam tugged on his few remaining tufts of hair, which signaled that he wasn't getting the results he wanted. As a professional film director, Adam was notorious for demanding take after take from actors, even for the simplest scenes. And he was hard on everyone, even firing extras for not fully embodying their characters' complex backstories.

Adam's directorial career consisted of a string of artsy independent films, and he experienced his share of difficult personalities and situations, but this project weighed the most on him. Unlike the past projects, this project needed to succeed. If a past film was unsuccessful, he attributed it to not being meant for the mainstream audience, or too intelligent for the viewers. Here though, he had to make something beautiful in its lack of elegance and massively popular among *AMHHV* viewers, who were the opposite demographic of any of his target audiences in the past.

The family watched in silence, all the way up to the double entendre at the end.

"Horrendous, truly horrendous," Adam scoffed.

"Goodness, Adam. Don't be so hard on everyone. I do agree this one won't do, however."

"Let the critiques begin, anyone want to start us off." Adam paused for just a half-second before unloading his criticisms. "Okay then, Eggplant."

"Yes Dad?" Eggplant eyes beamed with the very thought of his father addressing him.

"You were truly awful."

"Thanks Dad!" Clearly still excited that his dad was talking to him, Eggplant glazed over the harsh insult.

"I mean, right off the bat, when you open your present, I, oh, I didn't even mean to do that. 'Right off the bat.' I'm even clever when I'm not thinking. How hilarious!" Adam stared at his wife and son until Sarah forced a laugh. "Anyway, right when you opened your present, you looked happy, but not nearly as happy as you should be. The audience needs to buy in that this baseball bat is the best present you could ever receive."

"You could almost say that this gift was a home run," Sarah added, giddy with her own pun.

"Silence, Sarah, this is no time for that."

"But just 30 seconds ago you-"

"Please, please, please be a professional. This ain't the minor leagues."

To Sarah's befuddlement, Adam laughed at his own reference for a good ten seconds.

"Back to business. Eggplant, I mean, come on, I know I've said this before, but you just don't look happy enough. You gotta think of the happiest moment of your life and go there; otherwise we're not going to get the reaction out of you that we need."

"The happiest moment of my life is when we used to spend every Sunday together. I remember when we used to follow famous actors around town and sneak into pictures of them taken by the paparazzi. Or, when we used to go to the lake and feed ducks low-fat bread. We haven't done anything like that in years!"

"Eggplant," Adam shut his eyes with contempt, "I told you to think about the happiest moment in your life, not waste everyone's time by saying it out loud. Moving forward, next comment?"

"I'm sorry to say this, Adam, but your face just doesn't look convincing enough during the big crotch shot," Sarah admitted.

"Easy for you to say, being that you're not the one taking one to the privates."

"I know dear, I know. But if we're going to win this, we gotta go all out, we have to make sacrifices. You said it yourself, dear. I mean we are really close, it's not like it's going to take a lot of takes."

Adam looked straight down at his lap, as if holding a private meeting with his crotch. After 10 years of marriage, Sarah knew that Adam could never argue with or contradict himself. "Know what, Sarah, when you're right, you're right." Adam reached down into his pants and pulled his athletic cup right out of his pants and threw it on the table. "I'm in this to win this."

"Now it's my turn to bring something up. Sarah, I know you can see it, but I don't think you're connecting with your character."

"That's been bothering me for the last few takes, too. I'm really struggling with my assignment."

This caught Eggplant's attention, "But Mommy, aren't you just playing you?"

"Not just any mom, darling. I'm playing a loving mom."

Eggplant could tell his mom was struggling with the role of loving, responsible mom, too. His mom was an actress that practiced the method acting technique, where the actor lives their entire life as the character, for the duration of the film shoot. So for the last few weeks, Eggplant was the beneficiary of his mother's new role. For the last few weeks, his mom packed his lunch, walked him to and from school, and cooked a fresh meal for the family every day. For once, Eggplant felt like he actually had a mom.

"So, time for take seven?" Eggplant asked as he stood from his chair. Adam motioned him to sit.

"Buddy, go start cleaning up the room for the next take, we'll restart in 5, no, 4 minutes, exactly. I just need to talk with your mother about something."

"Okay. Hey Dad?"

"Yes?"

"I've been thinking-"

"Oh that's never good, but get on with it, chop chop."

"But Dad, isn't *America's Most Hilarious Home Videos* supposed to be real?"

"Yes Eggplant, please cut to the chase."

"Well, why are we pretending then? Isn't that cheating?"

"We already went over this, we tried to catch you doing something funny, Eggplant, but you're just not funny, or cute. Your mannerisms are so outdated and contrived, it's all been done before. Anyways, you're too old."

"But I'm only seven."

"Over the last 17 years of the show, the 9 grand-prize-winners that won because of child cuteness all had kids between two and four years old. You're past your prime, Egg. Now go to the other room, please. Start mopping the floor where the cake landed."

Eggplant complied and Sarah closed the door behind him.

"That take's not going to cut it," Adam said, outright. "The positioning is off, the lighting is dim, and the comedic pauses are off by a mile."

"We were oh so close this time, though."

"We don't need close we need perfect!" Adam slammed his fist on the table, instantly regretting his actions for a couple of reasons: one being he didn't want to act in a violent manner; and more immediately, it really hurt.

"Good heavens, did you break your hand?"

"I'm sorry Sarah, I didn't meant to, it's just the pressure has been getting to me lately."

"Oh it's okay, I've been stressed about this, too. If we don't win the whole thing, we'll never be able to repay our loans. Goodness knows what we will do next."

"We can't be thinking like that."

"Well we better soon, because we are going have to move out of Los Angeles County."

"We can't be thinking about this right now. Not yet. The day we move out of LA is the day we label ourselves as quitters."

"Oh Adam, we don't even live in LA anymore, remember? We had to sell our last house and now we're overpaying to stay in this pigsty of a place in Pomona. We move one town over and things are a lot cheaper."

We are not moving to San Bernardino County. End of discussion."

"We never should have made that *Out of Ink*, at least then our debt would be manageable."

"I said not to talk about this now!" Adam slammed his fist on the table again, this time he did not apologize. "We've made risks in the past. We were unlucky. That's not going to help us one bit right now.

We have an opportunity to make a lot of money right here. We need to focus."

"Dear, dear, you said *Out of Ink* was a great opportunity."

"That film was beautiful, okay, it was beautiful. We just got shut out because no one wanted to upset the balance of the almighty film industry and pick a one-person indy for an official selection. It was ridiculous. A complete mockery."

"We can't keep doing these takes, Adam; each take costs us: a frosted cake, wrapping supplies, a shirt, time. Don't forget about the time it takes us to set each one up. And the season finale is in 3 weeks, if we don't get our tape in soon, it won't even be reviewed until next season."

"I think you are acting out of character. I don't think housewives of the 50s disobeyed their husbands!"

"Goodness gracious, mothers of the 50s had to stand up for their families when the husband was away at war. You are away with your own dreams."

"What else are we supposed to do, Sarah? I hear a lot of complaining, but I haven't heard a better option out of you, not one!"

"Because you never listen, Adam! How do you think I feel? I'm the one that wanted to move north to Canada a few years ago! I saw they were growing in film jobs, we could have been making so much money right now. No wait, we could have been making money. Period."

"Canada? Our whole lives have been centered on making it in Hollywood. This is our dream to make it *here*, not in *Canada*, where they probably only make movies about hockey and maple syrup."

"I'd rather make hockey movies in Canada than be out of work and out of money here. All we have here is a dream, an empty one."

"It's not just the dream for us, it's our family's dream. We named our son after a freaking produce item."

When deciding to raise a child, Sarah and Adam were both well aware of the celebrity trend of naming children after fruit. However, by the time Sarah gave birth, all the attractive fruits and vegetables were taken up, leaving Eggplant as the best available option. They were the first to come up with Apple, Papaya, and even Corn as a distant back-up. But celebrity couples snatched up all the good names, one by one, until Eggplant was the least objectionable option.

"Well, my dear, now at least we agree on one thing. Dealing with the casting."

"We do?" Adam asked, surprised.

"Yes, as much as it pains me, Lord knows it's the right decision."

"Good, good. I'm glad you see it my way. And the replacement?"

"I texted his mother. He is on his way."

"Excellent. Time to break the news to Eggplant."

Eggplant was nearly done mopping up the floor when his parents finally emerged from the other room.

"Hi Mom! Hi Dad! Ready for try 7?"

"Yes, yes, Eggplant. But first, Mother and I would like to have a word."

"Okay. What about?"

Adam sighed and kneeled down to Eggplant's eye level. "Well, your mother and I have been talking. First, we just want you to know that you are our son, and we love you, and nothing will ever change that."

"I know that."

"You know that we love you very much."

"Yes, I know."

"And you also know how we were just talking about making sacrifices for the team."

"Yes."

"Even if that means something that can be potentially painful, like how I took out my athletic cup in order to give a more authentic reaction."

"You want me to get hit, too?"

"No, no, no. We're not talking about that at all."

Eggplant was relieved.

"But we both decided that you're not cutting it. We're going to have to recast your part."

"But I'm playing myself, Dad. You're going to replace me?"

"No, no, no Son," his dad smiled, "we could never replace you."

Eggplant smiled as his dad placed his hand on Eggplant's shoulder.

"We're just replacing you for this video, that's all."

"Why?"

"You're just not convincing enough."

"So you're rejecting me?"

"No Son, never. We would never, or could never, legally reject you as a son. We are just firing you as an actor playing our son."

"But at least I'm still your real son, right?"

"Of course Eggplant, of course."

"Oh wait," Sarah interjected. "With my character, I need to have one son, so for the duration of the show, I have to pretend you're not my son, but after that, of course you are our true son."

"Then, who's going to play me?"

The doorbell rang.

"Oh, speak about perfect timing," Sarah said as she rushed to the door, "Yep, he's here." Sarah peeled back the door, letting the brilliant rays of sunlight through as Eggplant's replacement walked through the door. Eggplant was very aware of his replacement and his bright blue eyes and his boyish smile. In walked Gil Firenhauser, Eggplant's nemesis.

"You replaced me with Gil Firenhauser? Again?" Eggplant was referring to the previous year's Q and U wedding, a hallmark kindergarten play where the letters Q and U marry to symbolize how the letters are always together. Eggplant thought that since his dad directed the play, he'd be a shoe-in for the role of U, the most enviable male role. But it was not meant to be, Gil was cast for the role of U and Eggplant was relegated to the role of L, which required Eggplant to tape a paper L to his forehead.

"Mom! Dad! How could you replace me with Gil?"

"Son, I mean, Eggplant, don't take it personally. We need to win this, and Gil gives us the best chance. I mean, look at those golden locks of hair. Americans go crazy for blonde kids."

As if on cue, Gil ran his fingers through his hair. "Yeah Eggplant, don't be offended. I'm just more talented than you."

With no role left to play, Eggplant plopped himself down on the stair steps as the new cast pulled it off in one take. Adam gave a most emphatic shriek of pain, Sarah gave her best impression of a loving mom, and Gil said his lines with double the cuteness that Eggplant could ever hope for.

O   O   O   O   O   O

Two weeks after submitting the video to *AMHHV*, the Zoobemans were notified via email that their video, titled *Baseball Birthday Bonanza*, was selected as a finalist for the May 13th show, which was the final regular weekly show before the grand finale. Eggplant sat in his parents' bedroom watching TV as they put the final touches on their attire.

In front of their bathroom mirror, Adam noticed Sarah was noticeably upset.

"Sarah, my love, are you okay?"

"Yes, I'm fine," Sarah replied, attempting to shrug off the inquiry.

"Sarah, what is it?"

"It's just, what if we don't win?"

"We've gone over this a hundred times. We can't lose. We are the perfect storm of comedy: we have a cute kid, a birthday celebration, a baseball bat, a dad taking a baseball to the groin, a freak accident with the cake, the cake falling on the dad's face, and a testicle joke at the end. We can't lose, we have everything. We are the perfect combination of everything that has ever won on this show. Not to mention a shot of a hot mom for eye candy."

"Adam," Sarah playfully slapped Adam's shoulder. Sarah tilted her head, motioning toward Eggplant, who was watching TV a few yards away.

"What? I'm not allowed to express how attractive I find my wife?" Adam grinned as he pulled his wife close. In her early forties, Sarah remained objectively hot. If it wasn't for their untimely pregnancy, she may have still been in Hollywood's eye for the diverse roles as *Hot Mom*, *Hot Single Mother*, or *Hot Teacher*.

They swooped in for the kiss, only to mutually pull away at the last second to abide by the cardinal rule: no touching or kissing of the face after the make-up is applied. They both returned to their perspective mirrors and rehearsed their lines for the softball questions they were to be asked during the show.

O   O   O   O   O   O

Eggplant saw his parents and Gil take off around 1 p.m. The taping was at 4, and their house was only 15 miles away, but his dad said he didn't want to risk being late in the traffic that had caused Eggplant's parents to miss so many of his recitals, soccer games, and *Bring Your Parents to School* days.

Eggplant returned to the living room where the TV was still on. The current channel was showing a movie called *The Truman Show*, starring Jim Carrey. Eggplant watched the whole thing, even though the glare on the TV was so great that Eggplant could see his reflection on the TV screen.

After the movie was over, Eggplant went into his parents' room. On the TV was a tape with *Out of Ink* written on it. Recognizing the title from his parents' countless arguments, Eggplant inserted it into the player and sat back.

Right away, Eggplant recognized the filming locations from the pictures around the house. It was their old home, before they had to move. The hour-long movie was very dull and only featured his mom, who occasionally took phone calls, but no other character was ever shown. It was about a cartoonist, played by his mom, who lost her job and was forced to teach herself graphic design in order to have a shot at another career. The character went on to become a decent artist, only to be rejected by every firm due to her old age. The movie ended anticlimactically, with Sarah's character remaining unemployed.

Unstimulated, Eggplant fell asleep dreaming of a world where everything was just an act. He woke up to his parents cheering as they came home, celebrating the video's first place finish at the show's taping. Two weeks later, they would return to the studio for the season finale.

O   O   O   O   O   O

So far, the night of AMHHV's grand finale unfolded as planned. From the season's pool of 26 weekly winners, *Baseball Birthday Bonanza* was selected for the *Funniest Four*, where the top three would leave with cash prizes and the fourth would leave empty-handed. The other three finalists included:

Summertime Splash: Starring a little girl who stands at the edge of a swimming pool and refuses to go in. Finally, the family's golden retriever runs up from behind and jumps into her back, pushing them both into the water.

Baby R Tired: A 30 second clip of a baby, probably 3 months old or so, falling asleep.

Fun-time Fiasco: While playing on the family's swing set, the dad's weight causes the swing set to break down and the dad's momentum carries him into dog poop.

All of the lights in the indoor arena formed an immense spotlight for the host, West Wayne.

"Welcome back, America. If you are just joining us now, this is the final round, the finale of *America's Most Hilarious Home Videos*. And now, it's time to find out who our grand champion is."

Wayne walked over to the family that shot *Summertime Splash*. "Hello family, you are the CHAMPIONS OF IT ALL!"

The family jumped up with pure joy, leaving the rest of the three contenders stunned.

"NOT!" Wayne yelled, with the same joyful enthusiasm.

The sarcastic pokes of the host, usually reviled by the Zoobeman family, were welcomed fully in this situation.

Now the *Summertime Splash* family was stunned. The tears of joy transformed into tears of despair.

"Gotcha guys! But seriously, you are our fourth place contestant. Bye-bye."

Adam wiped his brow and turned to Sarah as the fourth-place family exited the arena. "I told you they wouldn't win, having a private swimming pool in your video is a death sentence. America isn't going to vote for some upper-class family."

"Now for our second place contestant…*Funtime Fiasco!*"

Adam and Sarah both sighed with relief as Wayne conducted the exit interview with the *Funtime Fiasco* family. "Goodness Darling, I am about to have a heart attack."

"Stay calm, Sarah, we've got this," reassured Adam, "*Funtime Fiasco* was never going to win. Building a bad swing set shows irresponsible parenting. That's not good family values. Also, the gross factor of landing dog poop may have gotten them into the finals, but too many people are turned off by material that low-brow."

Wayne dismissed the family upon the conclusion of their interview and looked back at the camera. "From millions of submitted videos, two families remain. One walks away with a quarter million dollars and the other leaves with only $25,000. Now for the winner of *America's Most Hilarious Home Videos.* The winner of $250,000, or 25 million pennies, before taxes. Or the winner of 2.5 million dimes. The winner is…going to be revealed after the break."

A collective sigh rumbled through the audience.

Adam looked to his panting spouse. "Sarah we got this. We're going to win this."

"But sweetheart, how can you be so sure?"

"Please, we are going up against a tired baby. That always happens. There is nothing special about that. Our video, on the other hand, has everything a viewer could want."

"But the baby is so cute."

"You are forgetting the fact that the baby is ASIAN."

"What does that have to do with it?"

"Voters won't want to vote for foreigners like them."

"But I've heard them speak, they speak perfect English, better than most of the white people speak."

"Exactly, don't you see how that makes people uncomfortable? Americans are already angry at the Asians."

"What?"

"First they take away all the good manufacturing jobs-"

Adam's explanation was interrupted by the producer calling for silence since the show was back on air.

West welcomed the TV audience with his warm smile. "Alright, we are back from the break. For those of you that are just joining us, here's what you missed." This cued a 5-minute retrospective of what had happened during the previous 8-minute TV segment. Known for a steely demeanor, even Adam's anxiety was multiplying with every stall tactic instilled by the host. Finally, the retrospective concluded.

West applauded the clips, and reentered his speaking role. "Beautiful. Okay so this is for all the marbles. In one corner, we have the Zoobemans with *Baseball Birthday Bonanza*." The crowd showered the studio with thunderous applause.

"In the other corner, the Chow's with *Baby R Tired*." Equally loud applause was heard throughout. There was no clear-cut favorite video amongst the audience.

"Both are great videos, but remember, only one will leave with the first place prize of $250,000, and the other will leave with the third place prize of $25,000. Which I'm sure the Chows can calculate exactly how much smaller the third place prize is."

"Why would *we* know?" Mr. Chow asked.

"Please, I'm talking. So the winner is," Wayne again paused for seconds, "coming up after this break."

"YOU GOTTA BE FUCKING KIDDING," Adam shouted as he shot up out of his seat, his voice clearly audible over the hundreds of groans heard throughout the audience. Even Wayne heard his profane input, and walked over to Adam as soon as they were off the air.

"You better beeping watch it, you beephole, that beep-mouthed comment of yours just got broadcasted to the whole beeping world. This is a beeping family show." Previously made famous as a foul-mouthed comedian, nine consecutive years of hosting *AMHHV* had conditioned Wayne into never being able to curse, even in private.

The tirade from the show host stunned Adam for a second, but he regained his footing. "Shut up! You said you were gonna read the winner 20 minutes ago. Say who the damn winner is already."

"No beeping chance in beepin' beep, Motherbeeper. This is the beeping finale, and there are 100 beepin' million beepers just like you beepin' watching tonight. We make 2 beepin' million dollars for every 30-second commercial we beeping sell, so we're gonna milk this thing for all it's worth, Beep."

"Live in ten," said the show's producer, which put an end to the confrontation. Wayne walked back to the middle of the stage, dabbed sweat off his forehead, and stayed silent until the show came back on the air.

"Welcome back to the finale of *America's Most Hilarious Home Videos*!" West Wayne's genial smile returned. "There's no more commercial breaks folks. It is time to reveal the winner. In one corner, we have *Baby R Tired*, and in the other corner we have *Baseball Birthday Bonanza*. America has submitted a record-setting 230 million votes, and the winner is…"

Adam and Sarah grasped each other's hand tightly.

"*Baby R Tired*!"

The crowd blew the roof off the stage with exuberance.

Adam and Sarah sat frozen in time, not even breathing for moments, minutes. With his peripherals, Adam saw the *Baby R Tired* family spontaneously embrace in a raucous group hug, tears flowing from all of their faces. Even the baby, now just a year old, gave off a glistening smile.

"How did we lose?" Adam asked, not sure if his question was rhetorical. "We had everything," Adam said, aghast. "There's no way we lost."

A heavy hand landed on Adam's right shoulder. Adam rotated to his right to see a heavy-set man behind him in overalls and a farmer's cap.

"That's a tough break guys; at least y'all won $25,000, though."

"But we had everything: a cute kid, America's pastime, a hot mom, me taking a baseball to the groin and a cake to the face. We had everything a video could've had, and all they had was a baby falling asleep."

"Your video was damn funny, but nothing beats a baby falling asleep. That's just plain adorable."

"But how? There was absolutely nothing special about that. All babies get tired."

"Exactly," the man said as he put his arm around his boy on his right, probably around 13-14 years old. "Guess it reminds me of when Junior here used to fall asleep; once he even fell in his Cheerios. Too bad I didn't catch it on camera, then it would've been me standing up there in the winner's circle," the man said. His shoulders shook as he let out a hearty chuckle. "My son has made me so proud with his school accomplishments and his sports play, but I don't think I've ever been happier than when his head fell into that bowl."

O   O   O   O   O   O

Adam and Sarah awoke the next morning as if they had been asleep for years. Despite feeling a near-depression-like state the night before, the couple felt almost a sense of relief today. The $25,000 wouldn't solve all of their financial problems, which in a way solved all of their hard decisions. It wouldn't get them out of debt, but it would help them relocate. After cooking breakfast and walking Eggplant to school, Sarah began paying off delinquent bills and Adam searched for more affordable housing in nearby counties. Adam and Sarah only stopped when it was time to pick Eggplant up from school.

During their walk, Adam and Sarah agreed to surprise their son by taking him to the blockbuster film *Gigantic Poisonous Vaporizing Spider vs. Monstrous Zombie Shark*, which was exactly what it sounded like. When they revealed the surprise to Eggplant, he was so excited that it made them excited. Sarah now knew how her character felt in *Baseball Birthday Bonanza*. The family linked hands as they walked to the movie theater—which was no further than half a mile away. On their way, they decided to take a shortcut through the park which bordered the man-made lake where they fed the ducks years ago.

As the Zoobemans passed through the park, Eggplant tugged on his parents' arms and pointed. Eggplant was pointing to a mother duck and her ducklings playing in the man-made lake. The Zoobemans planted themselves on the nearest bench and watched the ducks for hours; not one of them realized they had missed the movie.

End of scene. Close curtains. Open Exit doors.

Melting Away Beneath Us

Hours I wait, hours upon hours of waiting, here, alone, on the ice, in the frigid cold that cannot be explained or imagined, only experienced, only suffered through. Even my thick fur is not enough to keep me warm. I'm still wet from my last plunge into the water an hour ago, my only close encounter of the day with a seal.

I stand on all fours, surveying three close holes in the ice. I've waited all day but I have no choice but to continue waiting. I have not eaten in days, and I'll only continue to get weaker. The sun is going down and I have one more shot to catch a seal. They can hold their breath for a while, but eventually, they have to come up. They can only stay below surface for about 10 minutes at a time.

I am here alone now. Great Bear caught a seal hours ago and dragged it back to his den where its skeleton is all that remains after the minor feast. Great Bear seldom travels home empty-handed, he is the top bear. He is the strongest, bravest, and smartest. Great Bear is my twin brother. He is superior to me in every category, and has been since the beginning.

The water in the hole straight ahead of me starts to tremor, something is coming up to the surface. I inch forward, a step away from the opening, so the seal cannot see me from under water. Moments later, the unknowing seal's head pops out of the water, eyes pointing in my direction. She sees me immediately and submerges instantly. Lunging forward into the water, I extend my paws for the retreating seal, nothing. Out of desperation, I dunk my head into the frigid water and snap at her with my jaws, catching barely an inch of her tail, shredding it as she swims away, wounded but alive. Trailed by a thin line of her own blood, she disappears in the murky water, too fast for me to pursue.

A few more hours pass, no more chances to catch seals come. Another failed trip. The miniscule shred of the seal's tail is still firmly lodged between my two teeth, a nagging reminder of what could have been and what should have been and what was not meant to be.

Too dark to see well, therefore too late to hunt, I decide to call it a day. I lumber in the way of the disappearing sun, to the mountainside, where I dig out some ice to lay in the hole. A lost day.

It is the morning and I am awoken by distressed roaring in the distance. It has been over a year but I know that roar. That is the roar of the mother of my children. She is in danger.

After mating, males are no longer involved with the females. The males do not take care of, protect, or feed the females, nor are the males involved with the raising of their children, often born as twins. Males go a lifetime without seeing their children. I know nothing is expected of me, yet I cannot distract myself from hearing her cry for help.

I can see her below, a few hundred strides in the distance, not too far from where I looked for food yesterday. Near her are two little ones, our cubs. I've never seen them before. Five strides from them is a much larger male, standing on his hind legs and snarling at her.

Male polar bears' lives consist of three tasks: mating, eating, and conserving energy, yet there was an urge to do something that strayed outside of those three tasks, despite my instincts, to save something that was mine. With no further hesitation, I break out in a sprint toward my family. The male is attacking them. He is trying to get to the little ones, my little ones. She refuses to back down, and continues to stand in his way, but he is bigger and faster and pushes her aside with ease. He keeps craning his neck, and snapping his powerful jaws, only to miss my cub's neck by a hair.

I close within a hundred strides of them and roar. They hear me and the male looks over for just for a second. He returns to his attack, this time more ferocious than before. He keeps clawing at her and extending his neck to snatch away my children but she doesn't let him, refusing to get out of his way.

I'm overheating but I keep sprinting. He slashes at her, knocking her to the ground. My cubs try to run but they can't outrun him. My cubs split and run in opposite directions. The attacker singles out the weaker cub and pursues him. It takes only a matter of a few strides for the attacker to catch up with the little cub. The attacker runs beside my little one and lowers his head with his mouth open. One snap of the jaw and it is all over. I roar again, disrupting him once again. But by the time he glances up, I am half a stride away from him, in mid-leap. He strains to get on his back legs, but I knock him down on his back. It is easier than expected, he is even thinner than me. Rolling back on his feet, he resumes his pursuit of my cubs, who both made their way to their mother. She struggled to roll off of her back, but now she is rejuvenated as he closes in and flashes her teeth at him. Even though she weighs half my size, the aggressive male is more scared of her than me. She is fighting to protect the very cubs she had sacrificed everything to protect and raise for over a year.

Now that the mother has fully recovered, the male realizes he has no chance. The cubs are safe behind their mother and I come up from behind the male. He looks at her, looks at me, and walks away with his head hung low.

We are safe for now. I walk over to her, the first time I have seen her since mating over a year ago. She is a little hurt, with a limp in her step, but she will be okay. The cubs hide behind her. They have never seen me before and do not know if I am a friend or an enemy. For all they know, I could have just fended the former intruder off so I could hunt down one of the cubs for myself. I walk right in front of her and put my nose on hers, then nuzzle my head to the right of hers so our heads are side-by-side, my left eye gazing into her left eye gazing back into mine. I feel her gentle breath on my left cheek and ear. This brief contact warms my entire body, even down to my heart, which had been frozen for the longest time. We stay like this for some time.

Through the corner of my eyes I see the cubs, my cubs, make their way out from behind their mother. She motions them in my direction. I tap their heads with my snout.

The winds change direction and I can smell a new scent. I may be older, slower, and weaker than most bears, but my sense of smell has become heightened, growing hand in hand with my desperation. It is probably some thousands of strides off, but the pungency and oily nature of the scent cuts right through the chill and the other odors I can detect. Such a scent could only belong to a whale. I guide my family toward the scent, in the direction of the still-rising sun.

5,000 steps later, we arrive at the carcass of the massive beast of a whale, five times longer than I am, beached on the rocks. The whale is on its side, with its right side against the sand. It must have been dead some time before it washed onto land. There are only three polar bears spread out around the belly of the whale and a handful of gulls standing on the beast's left side. I must have picked up the scent early.

The four of us start our feeding at the back of the whale, so as not to compete with the rest of the bears. The back is tough, and it is hard to break through the skin, especially for the cubs. After some time, neither cub succeeds, so I bend my knees to stoop to their level and gnaw through the whale's skin to the precious blubber. The skin is tough, but after breaking through, it is all oily blubber, perfect to replenish the lack of fat. My cubs are overjoyed with my help and bounce around with excitement at the sight of the blubber. It is nice to see my own work making my cubs so happy.

A couple of the bears finish feasting on the belly of the whale and depart, so we walk over to see if any of the nutritious parts of the whale remain. The other bears already ripped through to its insides. As I examine the contents of the whale's stomach, it is clear that the whale died with a full belly, but not with fish. Inside the belly of the beast are many pieces, some shine, some looking like thin kelp, and everything is very colorful with strange markings on them. A shiny piece, the color of blood, caught my eye. It was the size of a newborn otter pup. I've never seen or smelt anything like it before. The piece is light and easily fits in my mouth, but when I chew on it sharp pain cuts up my inner cheek and gums, forcing me to spit it out immediately. It was tougher and sharper than any bone I ever ate before. Luckily the bleeding is minimal and it should go away. My cubs eat some of the other scraps left behind.

It is not long until more polar bears arrive. The cubs' mother and I urge them to eat faster. It is best we leave before too long. There's still plenty of whale meat for everyone, but before too long the supply is going to get scarce, and the bears that join the feeding late are sure to get violent over their share of the diminishing meat.

Once the cubs, their mother, and I are beyond satisfied, we travel elsewhere. When we leave the carcass, twenty bears are feasting and more are closing in from every direction. Before we walk too far, I see another bear limping toward us on his way to the carcass. It is the male that attacked my family earlier. He looks at me and I look at him. He walks right past us.

We continue to distance ourselves. Our family is about to settle on a place to rest but we already can hear the echo of roars and violence over the wind so we decide to travel a little further and settle in a patch of ice. She lies next to me, facing me. The two cubs climb on me to sleep. One day ago I was starving to death, alone, and without hope. Now I am full, reunited with my family, and believe I can survive. I look at my cubs, my own creations. All I could ever want is with me right now.

After leaving their mothers, males spend their whole lives wandering their own ice kingdoms in solitude. They rule without fear of predators or danger, yet they rule alone, journeyers without a destination. Perhaps because they were lost and never would come across anything they would call their own again.

The next morning we resume our search for the next source of food. None of us are hungry, but we cannot depend on another whale beaching itself nearby. I can pick up the faintest scent for thousands and thousands of strides around, but I have failed to detect anything since the whale carcass.

We walk between massive temporary walls of ice on our right and a vast bay flowing into an even vaster ocean to our left. We are traveling on the big glacier, a hundred strides high. The walls we walk next to and the very glacier we walk on are enormous but temporary.

We all walk along the edge. To my left, I overlook the deep blue sea gulf below and over two thousand strides to my left is the gulf's opening, in between two giant mountains of rock and dirt. It was only two winters ago that the glacier went all the way to the two mountains.

My tail is nipped at. It's the little one. I remember when I was full of playfulness and youth. I start chasing him, to our right, away from the cliff. He's the slower of the two, but I take a while to catch him, enjoying the moment. After a couple dozen strides he is already tuckered out and rolls on his back as I come up to him and tickle his belly with my nose. I look back to her and Big Cub. She smiles at me. I return my attention to my son on the ground, to give him another nuzzle.

Crracckkk!

The ice is shattering beneath Little Cub and shatters between my left and right paw. With pure instinct, I shove my son left, the direction away from the sea as the cracking extends a hundred strides in either direction. The ice is breaking farther apart, the gap is increasing, and I leap over to safety. I turn back to the coast, but there's no sign of the other half of our family. The iceberg is already slanted too much. I fight every urge to jump on the falling ice mass to try to save them. Despite the urge, I restrain myself and watch the destruction below. They are gone.

Overcome with stress, I shake my head with vigor. The ice mass, a hundred strides tall, a couple hundred strides wide, and fifty strides deep, collides into the water, sending the biggest waves I have ever seen slamming against the still-attached ice. We are not safe here. I urge my cub to run away with me, as more broken ice is sent into the ever-increasing body of water.

We run until we know we are both safe. At least far enough before the ice beneath us would break off itself. My cub is scared to death, I don't blame him, I am ten years older than him and I am scared, too. This morning he had a mother, father, and twin brother. Now he just has me. He used to have a mother to take care of him, but now it is just me. An undersized male that cannot feed himself, I do not see any way where I would provide for this young one. It is hard to tell who is more afraid.

Male polar bears are meant to do three things, yet now we grieved, staring into the icy water. Without any eye contact, we both move on together.

My grief is only distracted by the faintest of scents found as the sun sets. The scent I pick up is the scent of walruses in the distance. It will take us the rest of today and half of tomorrow to reach them but we have no choice.

That night Little Cub snuggled underneath my stomach. I arched my back and put my arm around him, not allowing any distance between myself and what little I have left. Even if there is just an inch of separation, the ice would pull us apart.

Shortly after sunrise on the second day of our travel, we reached the gathering of walruses, located on a small island just a few dozen stroke swim from the beach my son and I are walking on. The collective steam from the 200 huddled walrus bodies forms a mountain that goes into the clouds above. The walruses huddle together on the other side of the island, away from us.

Little Cub and I swim over. Grown polar bears are known for being excellent long distance swimmers and have the endurance to swim for a day at a time. This brief swim offers no challenge to me but as I make my way onto the rocky beach, I see young Little Cub struggling a bit, but he makes it to shore.

As we catch our breath, I survey the colony of walruses resting a hundred strides away. In my years, I have never attacked a colony this large. Killing a walrus is quite an undertaking. The adult walruses are bigger than I am, and have sharp tusks as long as my arms. To successfully kill an adult, you have to sneak up on one when it is unaware of your presence, and pounce from behind and sink your teeth into the back neck and break through to the walrus's vitals. This is no easy task, since walruses are protected by a very thick layer of blubber and tough skin, and walruses are strong enough to pull themselves toward the water where they can swim away to safety.

Little Cub and I start walking toward the colony, singling out any walruses that may be sleeping, sick, old, or infants. With the colony still 50 strides off, a handful of walruses notice us and alert their kin of our presence with loud barks. With haste, the walruses begin making their way into the water. Even when rushed, walruses cannot move very fast, and I still have time to reach them.

We sprint the rest of the way, seeing that with every second, more of our prey escapes into the water where we are no match for them. Of all the massive bodies sliding toward the ocean, I see one that remains motionless, asleep. The sleeping walrus is larger than me and would still be even if I returned to my healthy weight. About half of the colony had retreated safely to the water, so I knew this was my best and, most likely, last chance. I run up from behind and climb up his back. I grip into his shoulders with my front paws and sink my teeth into the back of his neck, which wakes him immediately. With my entire force I try to dig into his skin, but I fail to even break through to the blubber. With me clenched down on top of him, the walrus steadily carries us both toward the water. I unclench my jaw and retry to penetrate the skin, but I fail again. The walrus attempts to shake me off, violently shifting his back. Despite my full effort, I slide off to the walrus's left side. I dig my paws into the sand and hoist myself onto the walrus's back, just to be shaken off again. The fringe of the rising tide tickles my paws and his flippers. We both know that the ocean is just a few steps away. I only have one more chance to bring him down, so I approach to his right side as he turns to me. I sink my teeth into him once again, but just as I am about to break through, a searing stabbing pain shoots through my right side. The walrus's right tusk punctures the skin over my right shoulder. I growl in pain and jump off of him to avoid his tusk sinking further into me. I'm left to watch him slide into the water.

My shoulder hurts and my walk is a bit impaired, but it's not as bad as it could've been. The puncture tore through to my shoulder, but did not penetrate into my lungs or heart. With no more walruses left on the beach, I am left to walk back to my son. The feast we shared a few days ago has worn off and both of our stomachs growl with hunger.

Now it is just my son and I. My eyes pan across the nearby landmass that we came from, full of nothingness and starving polar bears. Then I look in the opposite direction, to the endless view of sea and clouds. I know there has to be land somewhere on the other side of the sea, but I have no way of knowing exactly where it is or what is waiting for us. All I know is where we came from only holds despair and starvation. With my snout, I nudge Little Cub toward the water, in the direction of the endless sea.

As was before, Little Cub is hesitant to start swimming, but as we continue, he develops a better stroke and a stronger kick. The night comes, but we must keep swimming. The stars serve as a guide for us.

When the sun rises on the next day, we are still moving forward, but I have little energy. Little Cub swims for as long as he can, but as the day grows old, and the next moon comes, he swims for shorter and rests for longer. I join in with his exhaustion, floating on my back for longer lengths of time. Still no sign of land, just the occasional chips of ice, much too small to sustain our weight.

On the third sun of our swim, Little Cub is exhausted and can only swim a few strokes at a time. I too can only stroke so much before flipping on my back to take a rest. Polar bears are exceptional swimmer, and can swim for a week at a time if necessary, but that is under the best of circumstances. We are both starving and had very little fat reserves when we started this journey.

Seals swim around us, coming within a half body length from us. I swat at them twice before giving up. They are too fast to get caught and every pointless swipe is draining more of my depleted energy. The seals swim closer, with one even jumping over my back. They no longer fear us. We are no longer the kings of the ice. The seals eventually tire of playing around us and swim off as the next moon comes.

On the fourth day, Little Cub now exclusively rests on my back and cannot summon the strength to propel himself forward. The weight on my shoulders is impeding my progress yet is also the only thing keeping me going. Floating off in the far distance are larger chunks of ice, some big enough to hold Little Cub and I. My aching muscles churn a little faster knowing that temporary relief is seen on the horizon. Little Cub growls, and I see he's looking off to the right.

We are not alone. Six large black dorsal fins are spotted off to our right. A pod of orcas, known as killer whales, swim along a few hundred strides to our right. My heart rate rises. No orca has ever attacked a polar bear, but then again no seal has ever taunted a polar bear, either.

Sometime later the fins are still there. This is not a coincidence. The ice chunks are floating closer and closer, and my eyes do not deceive me for they are bigger than expected, with plenty of room for two grown polar bears. Yet we are not amidst the field of ice yet.

The orcas are coming closer now, as Little Cub and my swim takes us into a cluster of floating ice.

The orcas now branch out and encircle us. They are targeting Little Cub, weak and vulnerable. I roar a few times to scare them off, to little success. I've seen orcas hunt before, they try to separate the group and isolate the weakest member. Knowing this, I swim even closer to Little Cub, nothing will come between us. I swat my paws at any orcas that come too close.

As the circle of orcas shrinks around us and accelerates, Little Cub and I swim within reach of a larger ice sheet. The sheet is large enough for the two of us and we both climb on. At a minimum, I feel comforted, thinking that we've given ourselves time to rest as the orca pod swims off. After swimming couple hundred strides off in the distance, the orcas regroup and start swimming back toward our ice sheet. All six are swimming side by side and accelerate as they close in on our minimal shelter. When the formation is ten strides away, they arch their backs in unison, forming a wave that peaks in height right as it reaches our ice mass. My cub and I brace for the wave, barely able to sustain it. I manage to stay locked onto the ice, but Little Cub's front paws slip and he slides toward the edge of the ice sheet. His grip sets in right before he slides completely off, but shortly after, the ice splits down the middle, splitting us apart.

Again I am split from the one I love due to the ground crumbling beneath me. The orcas take turns peaking their heads out of the water. The orcas regroup, and clearly refocus on the smaller ice sheet holding my son. Once again the orcas reform formation, and swoop in. This time the wave is mistimed by a hair and comes in too late. Little cub stays sprawled flat against the ice and is unmoved by the wave. The pod will not miss again. I search our surroundings in the approaching darkness and see a much larger ice sheet to my right that is wider, longer, and thicker. We must make our way there.

The second time, the orcas do not make a mistake. The wave hits Little Cub at full speed and sweeps him off the ice with ease. With no time to think, I dive in to the water and swim in between my son and the orcas. The orcas reverse direction and swim back our way. My son is terrified for he has never been prey. I grab my son's arm with my left paw and drag him in the direction of the large ice sheet. Seeing us both in the water, the pod returns to circling around us, but we are able to climb atop the ice sheet, at least 15 body lengths long and wide, before they can get too close.

Little Cub and I plant ourselves in the middle of the ice sheet. Little Cub collapses on the ice, but I stand tall, not wanting to be caught by surprise again. The pod continues to swim away, but one orca breaks out of the circle and accelerates in our direction. The orca bursts out of the water and slams onto our ice sheet, sliding toward us with its mouth wide open. I shove my son to my left, out of the orca's path and narrowly avoid it myself by diving to the right. I swipe at the orca's side and shred deep into the skin as the orca passes by and reenters the water.

My sight stays focused on the retreating orca, and the trail of blood, as it rejoins the pod. Suddenly reminded of the danger polar bears possess, the pod swims off.

Little Cub nods off as I continue to watch the water deep into the night, not seeing any sign of the pod's return. After a while, I join my son and fall asleep, not knowing if I will ever see the sun again.

I am awoken by the faint glimmers of the morning light through the thick fog. The orcas must not have returned. My son still sleeps peacefully to my left, we survived the night. I stand up and walk around the ice sheet, still sturdy and intact. We remain weak, starved, and surrounded by water all around us. The foggy horizons around us look identical. Regardless, this is the best I've felt in a while, because all I need is my son by my side. I look back to him, the reason why I managed to swim that long and survive through everything. Little Cub opens his eyes, looking straight at me. The sun continues to rise behind my son as I stare back at him. The sunlight shines through the fog, and after I adjust my eyes to the light, I can see the first sign of land directly past Little Cub. Mountains, beaches, grass. I've never seen a more beautiful thing in my life.

About the Author

Didn't Know I Was Lost is the debut publication by Warren Pete. Warren writes in his spare time when not working full-time as a product and marketing manager for an app development company in Orange County, California. Warren's interest in current social issues, as well as his experience in entertainment, technology, and business, fuel most of his writing. Warren plans to publish his first full-length novel in fall 2014. To be the first to receive the latest publications, author news, and more, please visit warrenpete.com to sign up for the latest updates.

Warren would like to give special thanks to Natalie Chau and Stefani Peterson for their editing and advising throughout the entire process.

www.ingramcontent.com/pod-product-compliance
Lightning Source LLC
Chambersburg PA
CBHW060625130626
46555CB00002B/658